IN THE ITALIAN'S SIGHTS

BY

HELEN BROOKS

MILLS & BOON

First published in Great Britain 2012
by Mills & Boon, an imprint of Harlequin (UK) Limited,
Eton House, 18-24 Paradise Road, Richmond, Surrey TW9 1SR

© Helen Brooks 2012

ISBN: 978 0 263 89083 9

Harlequin (UK) policy is to use papers that are natural, renewable and recyclable products and made from wood grown in sustainable forests. The logging and manufacturing process conform to the legal environmental regulations of the country of origin.

Printed and bound in Spain
by Blackprint CPI, Barcelona

IN THE
ITALIAN'S SIGHTS

CHAPTER ONE

How had she got herself into this position? It was ridiculous, stupid—she wouldn't let herself think dangerous—and not at all like her. She was sensible, methodical—she didn't do the rushing off in an impetuous tantrum thing. She never had. Mind you, the impetuous tantrum depiction was her mother's definition of her actions, not hers.

Cherry Gibbs shielded her eyes as she stared up and down the narrow country road bordered by drystone walls with miles of olive groves stretching away as far as the eye could see in either direction. Then her gaze returned to the hire car, sitting stolidly in the warm May sun, the driver's door hanging open. For the umpteenth time in the last hour she climbed back in to the vehicle and tried the engine. Nothing. Not a murmur.

'Don't do this to me.' She pushed back a strand of silky brown hair from her hot face. 'Not here, not now. Please, please, *please* start this time.'

Holding her breath, she turned the key in the ignition. As dead as a dodo. The car clearly wasn't going to go anywhere. OK, what to do now? She couldn't sit here all day, hoping someone might come along. It wouldn't have been a problem if she had kept to one of the motorways or main roads, but after leaving the town where she'd stayed overnight she'd made the decision to get off the beaten track for a while. Italy, she'd found, was different from England in many respects—most of them good. But not with regard to driving.

In an unofficial sense, and to all intents and purposes, there were no rules of the road. Driving in the towns was a nerve-racking experience, and she'd found she needed her wits about her every second she was behind the wheel. Locals tended to pull out suddenly and without warning, overtake at hairpin bends, turn left or right on red lights if they saw an opportunity, keep bumper to bumper in their lane rather than give way to other drivers, and blast their horns incessantly if she sat at a green light for a split second.

She'd been in the region of Puglia, the southern 'heel' of Italy, for five days, and was in danger of developing a permanent stress-related headache. Somewhat ironic as she'd fled the UK to escape just that very thing. Hence the decision to give herself a break from the towns. Not that she hadn't enjoyed the last few days overall.

Since she'd arrived at the airport in Brindisi, and picked up the hire car she'd arranged to have waiting, she had explored the southern tip of Puglia, taking in Lecce and the Salentine Peninsula—which was undeniably beautiful. The compact, meandering Old Town of Lecce was a paean to Baroque artistry, every church façade positively dripping with stone representations of foliage, animal life and religious imagery, and when she had followed the coast road to the very tip of the land's end she'd felt as though she was on the edge of the world as she'd looked out from Santa Maria di Leuca across to the distant mountains of Albania. That had been a good day. She hadn't thought of Angela and Liam more than a dozen times.

After shutting her eyes tightly for a moment, she opened them and climbed out of the car. *No self-pity.* She gazed up into the brilliant blue sky. She had done enough crying over the last months to last a lifetime. This trip was all part of beginning her life anew—and that included no dwelling over the past or grieving for what she'd lost.

Reaching through the open passenger window she fetched out the map she'd bought at the airport and pored over it. She had left the little *pensioni* on the outskirts of Lecce after a late breakfast of cappuccino and sweet pastries, driving up the coast for some thirty-five miles or so before turning inland. She had stopped for diesel for the little Fiat in a town called Alberobello, famous for its gathering of quirky *trulli* houses—small limestone buildings with squat whitewashed walls and domed stone roofs. They were truly magical little houses, and she had seen others scattered here and there in the region. She had spent some time looking at them before buying a bag of figs and a *panetto*—a cake made with raisins, almonds, figs and wine—from a local market.

At least she wouldn't starve. She glanced at the purchases on the back seat of the car. It was beginning to feel like a long time since breakfast.

She'd left Alberobello some twenty minutes ago, and almost immediately had found herself in the heart of a traditional southern Italian lifestyle unchanged for decades, its landscape dotted with pine, almond and prickly pear trees and endless olive groves and vineyards. Alberobello had begun to batten down the hatches and shut up shop for the siesta as she had driven away, and she knew within minutes the place would resemble a ghost town, with empty streets and echoing alleyways bereft of any human activity. She would have been hard put to it to find anyone to help her in the town, much less out here in the middle of nowhere. She'd been following country roads and dirt lanes for a while and had no clear idea where the nearest village was.

Tossing the map back through the window, she sighed deeply. She had her mobile phone but who the heck could she call to get her out of this fix? No one at home could help, and there were no foreign embassies in Puglia—although she had taken the precaution before leaving the UK to get the number of the nearest embassy in Rome and the number of the British Honorary Consul in Bari. Neither of which were any use now, because she didn't have a clue where she was. Southern Italy had a justified reputation for petty crime and car theft in the towns and cities; bag-snatching was a possibility and she'd been warned not to leave the car in a dark or secluded place by the hire company and to keep any valuables out of sight. The very nice Italian man who'd delivered the car had also advised her to avoid walking alone late at night. Thieves could spot a tourist a mile away.

Still, she wasn't in a city or town here, was she? The thought was of little comfort. She had passed the odd tiny village and farmhouse, even the occasional *trulli* house since leaving Alberobello, but exactly how far she would have to walk before she reached the nearest habitation she wasn't sure—because she hadn't been concentrating on that. And she would have to take all her belongings with her. She winced at the thought. Her suitcase weighed a ton and even her shoulder bag was heavy. And it would mean leaving the car unattended. Think of all the red tape and paperwork if it got stolen.

Cherry sighed again. The olive groves either side of the road were picturesque, the warm balmy air was scented with summer, and the only sound was the lazy humming and buzzing of insects and the odd bird call; normally she would have drunk in such serenity.

Stupid car. She glared at it. But she wasn't going to panic. She would eat her lunch—it would be one less thing to carry, after all—and then start walking back whence she'd come. It was the only thing she could do. It might be hours, days, before someone came down this road, for all she knew, and the thought of staying with the car and it getting dark was a bit scary. She'd seen too many horror movies that didn't end well to do that. She smiled wryly at herself.

Cherry was sitting perched on top of the drystone wall eating the cake when she heard the sound of a vehicle. Narrowing her eyes, she peered into the distance, her heart pounding. She saw a cloud of dust first, on the road in front of her. If it was one of the local farmers he was going to be thrilled to bits with the roadblock she'd inadvertently caused. Nevertheless, a middle-aged fatherly farmer would be preferable to one of the many Don Juans she'd encountered since being here, who clearly considered a young English girl on her own fair game. It didn't help that she looked so much younger than her twenty-five years either. Small at five-foot-four, and naturally slender, she was resigned to being taken for seventeen or eighteen. Liam had often pulled her leg about it, saying he was aware everyone would think he was cradle-snatching when she was constantly asked for her ID at nightclubs.

She could see a car now, and all thoughts of Liam

went out of her head as she surveyed the midnight-blue Ferrari nosing its way towards her. Hell. Definitely one of the local Lotharios. And no doubt one who'd think he was doing her a great honour by brightening up her sad existence and offering to sleep with her—like the one a couple of days ago, who'd asked her if she'd like some real Italian *loooove*. She'd actually laughed at the way he'd drawn out the last word, before refusing his generous offer as politely as she could. He'd taken the rebuff with the lazy, philosophical good humour most young Italian males exhibited towards the opposite sex, joining his friends after blowing her a theatrical kiss. Not for the first time since she had been in Italy, she'd thought the outrageous flirting was just a game. Albeit an ever hopeful one.

Cherry clambered down from the wall, brushing crumbs of cake from her T-shirt. She had reached the Fiat by the time the approaching car drew to a halt. The tinted windows made it difficult to see the occupant, and as the driver's door opened she braced herself, trying to gather her composure. It was one thing dealing with over-confident and amorous males in the safety of crowded streets or market places—quite another on a lonely stretch of road without a soul in sight. For a split second all the stories she'd ever heard about women tourists abroad getting raped or murdered were as one in her mind.

The man who uncoiled himself with leisurely ease from the Ferrari was no youth. Cherry had a quick impression of height—at least six foot—breadth—his shoulders were broad and strong—and a handsome dark face which had lines of experience carved into it, before he drawled something in Italian. She didn't understand any of it beyond the *signorina* at the end.

'I'm sorry, I don't speak Italian,' she said quickly.

She thought he sighed before he said, 'You are English?'

It was said with an air of resignation. He didn't actually add, *Another stupid tourist*, but he might as well have. Cherry felt her hackles rising and her nod was curt.

'So.' He surveyed her through dark sunglasses. 'There is a problem, *signorina*?'

Yes—and she had the feeling she was looking at it. With a calm she was far from feeling, Cherry gave a cool smile. 'I'm afraid my car has broken down.'

'And your destination?' he asked smoothly.

'I don't know.' That sounded ridiculous, and she hastily added, 'I was just exploring. I wasn't making for anywhere specific.' That didn't sound too great either.

'Where are you staying?'

This time she kept her voice firm and precise when she said, 'I've been staying in Lecce, but I decided to come up the coast for a while. To do a bit of sightseeing,' she added defiantly.

'This is not a coast road, *signorina*.'

Sarcastic swine. 'I'm aware of that,' she said crisply. 'Someone told me about the medieval castles of Puglia, and in particular the Castel del Monte. I—I was going in that direction, but I wanted to see a bit of the countryside.'

'I see.' The two words told her exactly what he thought of her decision to turn inland. 'And now you are blocking my road.' He moved slightly and every nerve in her tensed.

'*Your* road?' she asked warily.

'*Si,*' he said with silky gentleness. 'This is my estate

you are on, *signorina*. Did you not see the sign some distance back, telling you you were on private land?'

Oh, great—perfect. No, she hadn't seen his stupid old sign. 'There was no gate,' she said defensively, skirting his question.

'We have no need of gates. In Italy we respect one another's property.' The message was abundantly clear.

She *really* didn't like this man. 'Well, I'm sorry,' she said tersely. 'I can assure you that if I had known it was *your* land I wouldn't have set foot on it.' The words themselves could have been an apology. Her inflexion made them anything but.

To add insult to injury, she was sure she saw the stern, faintly sensual mouth twitch with amusement before he walked over to her, saying, 'So, let us see if we can persuade your car to continue its journey. The keys?'

'They're in the ignition.'

In spite of her predicament, Cherry found she was praying the car wouldn't make her look even more of a fool by starting immediately—but she needn't have worried. After a moment or two he released the bonnet and peered in, then tried the engine again. Still nothing, she thought gratefully.

Sliding out of the car with the natural gracefulness all Italian males seemed to have, he said mildly, 'When was the last time you filled up with petrol, *signorina*?'

Ha! She had him there. She wasn't so dopey she'd run out of fuel. 'Today,' she said triumphantly. 'Before leaving Alberobello. I've got a full tank.'

'And after you had bought the fuel? Did you leave the town immediately?' he asked quietly.

She stared at him. She had no idea what he was getting at. 'No. I filled up with diesel and then explored a bit.'

'On foot?' And, as she stared at him, 'On foot, *signorina*?'

Was that a crime? 'Yes, on foot.' Now he was closer she was finding his maleness somewhat intimidating. The sculptured bone structure of the handsome face, the thick, dark hair slicked back in a severe cut and the clearly expensive clothes he was wearing all contributed to a slightly predatory arrogance that was unnerving in the present circumstances.

He nodded slowly. 'I think, perhaps, you have been the victim of one of the—how do you say in England?—the scams that are prevalent in the cities and towns. A full tank of fuel is worth stealing.'

'Stealing?' she echoed. Even to herself she sounded witless.

'*Si, signorina*. It is relatively easy to make a small hole in the petrol tank and syphon off the liquid into a suitable container.' He shrugged, Latin-style. 'It is an inconvenience.'

And how. Glaring at him as though he'd done the deed himself, Cherry said acidly, 'So in Italy this respect of property you talked about doesn't extend to cars, Signor…?'

'Carella. Vittorio Carella.' He smiled, apparently not in the least put out by her sarcasm. 'And your name, *signorina*?'

'Cherry Gibbs.' It sounded dull and terribly English in comparison. Italian names were so beautiful, so romantic.

'Cherry?'

He frowned slightly and she found herself wondering what colour his eyes were behind the dark glasses. Brown, she guessed. Or deep ebony. Possibly hazel. She'd seen quite a few Italians with hazel eyes over the last days.

'Like the fruit?' he asked softly.

She inclined her head. 'My mother apparently had a craving for cherries all the time she was carrying me, and so…' She'd often thought she ought to be grateful it hadn't been bananas or strawberries. She didn't add that her second name was Blossom—something her mother had thought extremely witty at the time, apparently, but which had caused her to be endlessly teased at school. Parents never seemed to think of things like that.

'You do not like your name?' he said, in response to her tone of voice. 'I think it is charming.'

He took off his glasses as he spoke and she saw she'd been wrong about his eyes. They were grey. A deep, smoky grey framed by thick curly lashes that might have looked feminine on a less masculine man but on him were positively spellbinding.

'So, Cherry, I think we have established your little car is going nowhere for the present. Is there someone you wish to call to come and pick you up? Your parents, perhaps?'

Before she had considered her words, she replied, 'I'm not here with anyone.' Then wished she'd bitten her tongue.

The beautiful eyes narrowed. *'No?'* He was clearly shocked. 'You are a trifle young to be abroad on your own.'

Same old syndrome. He clearly thought she was just out of gymslips. 'I am twenty-five,' she said crisply. 'More than old enough to go where I want, when I want.' She could see she had surprised him. But then to be fair, she reasoned, today—with her hair loose and tousled, and dressed in old cotton trousers and a baggy T-shirt—she looked even younger than usual.

He recovered almost immediately. 'You clearly have good genes,' he said smoothly. 'My grandmother is the same.'

Cherry found she didn't like being compared with his grandmother, although she couldn't have said why.

'You have the number of the hire company?' he said practically.

She nodded. It was in her bag, with her passport and other papers. It took her a minute or two to dig it out. She found she was all fingers and thumbs with those grey eyes trained on her. Eventually she had it. The number was engaged.

'No matter.' It was impatient. 'You can try again from the house. What do you need to bring with you?'

'The house?' She was doing the parrot thing again.

'*Si*, my house. You cannot stay here.'

She wasn't going anywhere with him. 'Look, I'm sorry I'm blocking your road,' she said quickly, 'but once I get through to the hire company they can send someone to collect the car and give me a different one. Is—is there another way for you to get out?' she finished hopefully.

He didn't answer this. What he did say—and with an air of insulting patience—was, 'It could be hours before you are in a position to leave, Cherry. They may not have another vehicle available or be in a position to collect this one. It might be tomorrow before this can be arranged. Do you intend to spend the night in the car?'

That was infinitely preferable to spending it in his house. 'I wouldn't dream of imposing on you,' she said stiffly. 'I'm sure I can find a small hotel or guest house somewhere close.'

The grey gaze took in her bulging suitcase and the equally bulging shoulder bag. 'It could be a long hot walk,' he said silkily, 'with nothing at the end of it. I would not recommend putting yourself in such an unnecessarily vulnerable position when there is no need.'

No need was relative. The way he'd said her name, in that delicious accent, and the fact that he was easily the most attractive man she'd seen since she couldn't remember when, as well as being the most arrogant, was acutely disturbing. It was ridiculous, but the sooner she was well clear of Vittorio Carella the better she'd feel.

On the other hand the suitcase weighed a ton, the sun was beating down, and once she was clear of the Carella estate she'd be at the mercy of any Tom, Dick or Harry she happened to meet. Or the Italian equivalent. 'I'll try the number again,' she prevaricated. It was still engaged.

Vittorio was leaning against the car's little bonnet, his arms folded and the sunglasses in place once more. She wondered how such an outwardly relaxed stance could express so much irritation. He clearly relished this situation as little as she did. Forcing herself to speak calmly, she said, 'Perhaps if I could take advantage of your hospitality for an hour or two while I sort things out?'

'Of course.' Within moments he had transferred the luggage to the Ferrari, locking the Fiat and then opening the passenger door of his car for her to slide in.

Conscious that she was riding in a Ferrari for the first—and probably the last—time in her life, Cherry sank down in the cream leather seat. The car was sleek and magnificent—much like its owner, Cherry thought with a touch of hysteria. When he joined her in the car her senses went into overdrive. The muscled body was big, he was wearing an aftershave which was sex in a bottle, the gold Rolex on one tanned wrist shouted wealth and authority, and she had never felt so out of her depth in all her life. It was an acutely uncomfortable sensation.

'OK?' He glanced at her as the car's engine purred into life like a big cat, and then they were travelling backwards far too fast—in Cherry's opinion, at least—there being no room to turn round in the narrow, dusty road.

Her heart in her throat, she watched the drystone walls flash past and prayed she'd live to see another day. He was a madman. He had to be. Or a racing driver? No, a madman.

It was another few minutes before a passing place in the road enabled Vittorio to turn the car round in the most perfectly executed three-point turn Cherry had ever seen, and by then she had realised Vittorio wasn't a madman—just the best driver she had ever come across. It was as though he was part of the powerful machine as he handled the Ferrari with a skill which was breathtaking. But then if anyone should be at home in a Ferrari it was an Italian.

'You—you like driving?' she croaked out once they were facing the right way and she'd managed to unclench her hands.

'*Si,*' he agreed easily as the car leapt forward. 'It is one of the pleasures of life that carries no sting in the tail.'

She would have asked him what he meant by that, but she'd just caught sight of the incredible house in the distance, nestled within an expanse of century-old olive groves. She had found since being in the region that this land of olive groves and vineyards, surrounded on all sides by a balmy if slightly craggy coastline, held white-washed buildings on the whole, which glistened in the sunshine. The house they were approaching was built of a honey-colored stone, however, its pale walls glowing in the afternoon sun and its grey stone roof benign and tranquil. Balconies, bright with trailing bougainvillaea, surveyed the olive groves with sleepy ambience, and several large pine trees stood as sentinels either side of the sprawling building.

'Casa Carella,' Vittorio drawled lazily, noticing her rapt gaze. 'One of my ancestors built the main house in the seventeenth century and subsequent Carellas have added to it.'

'It's beautiful,' she breathed softly. As they came closer she could see just how beautiful. And how large and imposing.

Vittorio brought the Ferrari to a stop and smiled as he turned to face her. She wondered if he knew how that smile affected the opposite sex and then decided that of course he did.

'Grazie.' His eyes moved from her face to the languid villa. 'I, too, think my home is beautiful and have never wished to live anywhere else.'

'Do you still farm the olives?' she asked weakly, reeling from the way his smile had softened the handsome but somewhat stern features.

'But of course. The production of olive oil is one of the oldest industries in Puglia, and the Carella estate is second to none. Because of the methods required to harvest and produce the oil it is impossible to turn the industry into a high-tech affair, however. Modern machinery may be used, but the industry here is still by and large a private one, with the families of farmers tending to their own trees and producing their own oil as opposed to giant conglomerates. I like this.'

He turned to look at her again. 'My great-grandfather

was first and foremost a businessman, though, and invested much of the Carella wealth here and there, making sure we were not solely dependent on the olive trees. He was—how you say?—an entrepreneur. Is that correct?'

Cherry nodded. So he was one of the filthy rich.

'He was, I understand, a formidable man, but his ruthlessness guaranteed a privileged lifestyle for future generations.'

She stared into the dark face. He sounded as though he approved of his great-grandfather's hardness. 'You think ruthlessness is a good thing?' she murmured.

Slate-grey eyes met her blue ones. 'On occasion, *si*.' He opened his door before she could comment, walking round the low bonnet and helping her out of the car.

Cherry found she didn't want him to touch her. It evoked something of a chain reaction which had her nerve-endings quivering. Not that he prolonged the contact. Once she was standing on the pebbled forecourt which led to wide circular steps fronting the house he stepped back a pace.

'I am sure you would like to refresh yourself,' he said formally, reminding her how bedraggled she must appear to him. 'One of the maids will show you to a guest room and I will have coffee and cake waiting when you are ready.'

The door to the villa had opened as he'd spoken, and a neat little uniformed maid was standing in the aperture.

'Ah, Rosa.' He gestured for Cherry to precede him up the stone steps and she found she'd forgotten how to walk. 'Would you take the *signorina* upstairs to one of the guest rooms and make sure she has everything she needs? And perhaps you would like me to try the hire company for you?' he added to a bemused Cherry, who was trying not to gape at the palatial interior.

The light, cool hall, with a marble floor and white walls hung with exquisitely framed paintings, was huge, its air scented with bowls of fresh flowers and several chairs and tables dotted about the vast expanse. And the staircase stretching in front of them was a thing of beauty in itself, made of the same pale green marble as the floor and curving upwards to two levels, giving the impression that the hall itself was an inner courtyard.

Speechless, she followed the maid up the stairs and halfway along a landing, whereupon the young girl opened a door, allowing Cherry to precede her into a vast bedroom. 'Please to call if you need anything, *signorina*,' the maid said in broken English as she walked across and opened the door to an *en-suite* bathroom. She waved at open basketwork shelves holding neatly folded fluffy towels and toiletries and then left the room, shutting the door quietly behind her.

'Wow!' Cherry breathed out softly as she stood surveying her surroundings. The cream, stone and taupe colour palette of the room was offset by the blaze of colour coming from the open full-length windows leading on to a balcony thick with purple, red and white bougainvillaea and holding a small table and two chairs. It was obviously a guest bedroom—there were no personal belongings of any kind when she furtively opened one or two of the doors of the wall-to-wall wardrobes and drawers. Imagine what the rest of the house must be like, Cherry thought weakly. She'd been right. He must be absolutely loaded.

She padded across to the balcony. It overlooked an enormous garden stretching away from the back of the villa for what seemed like miles to her stunned gaze. It was bursting with tropical trees and shrubs and manicured flowerbeds, and the ancient walls which enclosed the garden from the olive groves were brilliant in places with cascade upon cascade of more bougainvillaea. An Olympic-size swimming pool glittered blue under the clear cerulean Italian sky, and orange, apricot, almond and fig trees lived in harmony in a small orchard at the very rear of the grounds. She had never seen anything like it.

Double wow! She breathed out slowly. Triple. What an oasis. How the other half lived!

As she continued to gaze out she noticed what must be Vittorio Carella's gardener, tending a flowerbed next to a lush flower-covered bower, but otherwise the sun-soaked grounds were still, slumbering in the heat of the afternoon.

One thing was for sure, Cherry thought with wry humour as she stepped back into the bedroom. Vittorio Carella was no ordinary olive farmer. And she supposed if she had to be stranded anywhere for a few hours she could have picked somewhere a darn sight worse than Casa Carella.

Becoming aware she had been lost in contemplation when she should have been freshening up, Cherry hastily walked into the gorgeous *en-suite* bathroom of cream marble. The mirror which took up all of one wall showed her just how grubby and bedraggled she looked. She groaned softly. No wonder he'd thought she was a young kid playing at being grown-up. Urgent repair work was needed.

The bathroom held everything from hairbrushes and cosmetics—still in their wrapping—to male and female

perfume and other such niceties. Clearly the guests of
Vittorio Carella had their every need met. But she wasn't
a guest. Not in the traditional sense anyway.

Cherry stood in front of the mirror, decorum warring
with vanity. Vanity won. After washing her face, and
brushing her hair until it shone like silk with one of the
brushes she'd unwrapped, she opened a tube of mascara
and a pot of eyeshadow. Not for the first time she blessed
the fact she was a female and had make-up at her disposal. She might have entered the house as a little lost
waif and stray. She certainly didn't intend to leave as
anything less than a full-grown woman!

CHAPTER TWO

WHEN she opened the door of the bedroom to go downstairs the little maid was hovering at the end of the landing, fiddling with the huge bowl of sweet-smelling roses on a small table under the magnificent arched window which flooded the space with light. Cherry smiled at her.

'Ah, *signorina*. If you will come this way? The *signore*, he is waiting,' the young girl said politely.

Cherry nodded and followed the immaculately dressed maid as she led the way down the stairs and across the hall. After knocking on a door the girl opened it and then stood aside for Cherry to enter. The drawing room was even more beautiful than she'd prepared herself for: the ceiling high, the light wood floor scattered with thick rugs, the gracious furniture and drapes clearly wildly expensive and the white walls covered with exquisite paintings. The huge French windows were open to the scents of the garden beyond, and on the patio immediately beyond the windows a fountain tinkled in the afternoon heat.

But all this was on the perimeter of her consciousness. Her senses were caught up with the man who had risen from an armchair at her entrance and was now saying, 'Come and sit down and take some refreshment. Would you prefer coffee or perhaps a cold drink? Orange juice? Pineapple? Mango?'

'Coffee will be fine, thank you.' He remained standing as he waved his hand at a chair opposite his. A coffee table was groaning with an array of cakes and pastries, and the aroma from espresso coffee was rich. His loose-fitting trousers and silver-grey cotton shirt were clearly expensive, and the way they sat on the lean male body was guaranteed to make any female heart beat a little faster.

He didn't sit down again until she was seated, and then he poured her a coffee before gesturing at the cream, milk and sugar. 'Help yourself.'

'Thank you. I take mine black.'

'It is the only way.' He smiled in agreement.

Her heartbeat—which had just returned to normal—quickened again. He really was the man with everything, she thought weakly. It was a shame that included an ego to match.

He picked up the cakestand and offered it to her, and as she gazed at the sweet delicacies she found she was hungry. She selected one of the small iced sponge cakes filled with cream and jam which she knew were called *sospiri*—sighs in English—and sighed herself inwardly. What must it be like to enjoy such a privileged life, free from the cares and trials which afflicted most people? He only had to crook his little finger and his every need was catered for. Heady stuff to the uninitiated.

'I spoke with the hire company while you were upstairs, but they will not be able to send another car for twenty-four hours.'

Cherry almost choked on the cake. 'Twenty-four hours?'

'This is not a great problem, surely? You had no pressing engagement?' he asked with silky smoothness.

He knew she didn't. 'No, but—' She paused, wondering how to say she had no intention of staying in this house for twenty-four hours—if that was what he was suggesting. 'But I can't impose on your hospitality—'

'Please do not speak of it. You are more than welcome to stay for as long as you like. I am desolate you have had such a bad experience whilst visiting my beautiful country. Let me make amends by offering you the safety of my home until the new car arrives.'

Oh, hell. What could she say to that?

In the event she wasn't called upon to say anything, because the drawing-room door opening with a flourish caused both their heads to turn to the voluptuous young woman standing in the aperture, her hands on her hips and her eyes flashing fire. Cherry didn't need to speak the language to understand the thrust of the outburst in Italian which followed. For some reason the girl was furious with Vittorio, and not afraid to tell him so in spite of his darkening face. Cherry found she was beginning to enjoy herself.

He rapped out something in Italian which stopped the flow but still left the girl glowering at him. Then he turned to Cherry. 'I apologise,' he said with steely flatness. She could see he was hanging on to his temper by a thread. 'My sister is not usually so bereft of manners. Let me introduce you. Cherry, this is my sister, Sophia. Sophia, meet Cherry, a guest from England who deserves more courtesy than you have shown.'

Cherry could see Vittorio's sister was fighting for control but now she stepped forward, forcing a smile as she held out her hand and said, 'I am sorry. I did not know

Vittorio had anyone with him or that we were expecting a guest.'

A little embarrassed now, Cherry smiled back. 'You weren't expecting me,' she said awkwardly as she shook hands. 'I'm afraid I strayed on to your property by mistake and my car broke down, so it's me who should be apologising for intruding.'

Vivid green eyes set in a face which was quite outstandingly lovely surveyed her for a long moment. And then Sophia smiled—a real smile this time. 'No, it is me,' she said ruefully. 'But you are most welcome, Cherry from England. Where is your car?' she added. 'I did not see it.'

Cherry waved her hand vaguely in the direction of the road. 'Out there somewhere. I'm afraid it's blocking the way to the house. Apparently my petrol was syphoned off in the last town.'

'The south road?' Sophia enquired of her brother, who nodded, his face still grim. 'It is of no matter, Cherry. We have more than one entrance to the property. You are staying for dinner?' she added.

'Cherry is staying overnight until the hire company can deliver a new vehicle.' Vittorio's voice was cold.

'Then I will see you later. I am going to my room to rest.' Sophia swung round, her hair—which hung in a glossy black curtain to her waist—rippling as she left the room.

Cherry sat down again, reaching for her coffee cup and not knowing what to say. Clearly brother and sister were at loggerheads over something or other. Aiming to relieve the crackling atmosphere, she murmured, 'Your sister is very beautiful.'

'And very wilful.' It was almost a bark. And then he

raked a hand through his hair. '*Scusi*. Now it is I who has
the bad manners, *si*? But Sophia—she tries my patience.'

Cherry had the feeling that patience was not one of
Vittorio's attributes at the best of times. He had the air of
a man who was used to having people dance to his tune
without question—a man who controlled his world absolutely. She found all her sympathies were with his sister,
whatever the disagreement was about. Quietly, she said,
'I don't think it's necessarily a bad thing for a woman to
be strong and wilful. We are living in the twenty-first
century after all.'

He looked at her. A hard look. 'How old do you think
my sister is?' he asked expressionlessly.

Taken aback, Cherry hesitated. 'My age? Twenty-five
or thereabouts?'

'Sophia will be seventeen on her next birthday in four
months' time,' he said grimly. 'And although she has
the body of a mature woman I can assure you she has
the mind of a sixteen-year-old—a reckless and obstinate
sixteen-year-old. Our parents died when she was still very
young and I have been her guardian since then, but over
the last few years it has been a battle.'

Teenage girls. She could have told him it wouldn't be
an easy ride—not with rampant hormones and especially
not with someone who looked like Sophia. The boys must
have been after her in droves since she was out of nap-
pies.

He confirmed this with his next words. 'There is a
boy,' he ground out woodenly. 'She has been meeting him
secretly when she was supposed to be with schoolfriends.'

'But that's natural at her age.'

His mouth compressed. 'Sophia is a Carella. She
knows there will be no boys until she is eighteen, and

then only when she is chaperoned. To do such a thing is unforgivable.'

Cherry stared at him. 'That's ridiculous.'

'In England, maybe. Not in Italy. Not among girls of good families. She has attended a select school where the girls are supervised at all times. When she is eighteen any suitors will come to me first. This is for her protection.'

He couldn't be serious. What a dinosaur!

'My housekeeper now has to accompany her when she leaves the house as I cannot trust her. It is an inconvenience.'

No power on earth could have stopped Cherry's next words. 'And what about her? Sophia?' she asked indignantly. 'She must be feeling so embarrassed if she has to see her friends with your housekeeper tagging along. That's cruel.'

Stormy grey eyes turned thunder-dark. She watched him rein in his temper and gain control, and it was impressive. 'You are a guest in my home, *signorina*.' He was suddenly very much the aristocrat. 'I must not burden you with my concerns. Suffice to say Sophia is a child and must be protected from herself. Now, if you will excuse me, I have business to attend to. Please make yourself comfortable and ring for anything you desire. The pool and grounds are at your disposal, of course, and dinner is served at seven o'clock.'

He had swept out of the room before Cherry could think of a reply. Although once the door had closed behind him a hundred acidic put-downs were there.

What a horrible, arrogant, chauvinistic pig of a man— and his poor sister, she thought angrily, her cheeks burning. Sophia was virtually kept in a cage here. Albeit a gilded one. He was still living as though it was two or three centuries ago, when women had no rights nor voice of their own.

Cherry sat and brooded for another ten minutes, absent-mindedly eating three more of the delicious cakes and pastries, which were the best she'd tasted since arriving in Italy. The scents of a thousand flowers drifted into the room from the open windows. The patio area was bright with huge terracotta pots of lemon-scented verbena, pink begonia, brilliant red geraniums, salvias, pelargoniums and other flowers she didn't recognise but which all added to the dazzling display of summer colour. Suddenly she wanted to be outside, despite the afternoon sun. A dip in that magnificent pool would be sheer heaven.

Decision made, she left the drawing room and found her way to her bedroom, where she changed into the modest black one-piece swimming costume she'd brought with her. She had also packed two brightly coloured bikinis, both of which were on the skimpy side, and she balked at wearing those here. It was silly, but somehow the thought of appearing half-naked anywhere within a ten-mile radius of Vittorio was out of the question. To that end she pulled on a brightly coloured sarong which went with one of the bikinis for good measure, feeling better once her legs were covered.

She sat down on the bed once she was ready, gazing round the room as she admitted to herself she was feeling a mite guilty about the way she'd behaved. It *had* been good of Vittorio to offer her refuge the way he had, and she didn't think she had actually thanked him once. She bit her lip, her small white teeth gnawing at the soft flesh. It wasn't like her to be so antagonistic—just the opposite, in fact.

She shook her head at herself, her shoulder-length brown hair, which the Italian sun had bleached almost blonde in places, shining like raw silk.

But it was him. Vittorio. He'd rubbed her up the wrong way from the minute she'd laid eyes on him—or certainly from the first time he'd opened his mouth. He was so arrogant, so sure of himself, so very *male*. But that didn't excuse her ingratitude. She'd have to apologise and thank him properly for coming to her rescue. She groaned softly, wriggling off the bed and standing up. But after her swim. Maybe tonight during dinner? And then once the replacement car arrived tomorrow she'd thank him again for his hospitality and put as many miles between them as she could.

She slipped on the daisy flip-flops she'd bought for the beach and walked to the door, turning round and looking at the sumptuous room again before she left. The whole situation she found herself in seemed quite surreal: one of the most—if not *the* most—handsome men she'd ever seen in her life, a house and gardens straight out of the pages of a glossy magazine featuring millionaire lifestyles, servants, wealth, splendour, and here she was, bang-smack in the middle of it. Even if it was just for a night. She almost felt like pinching herself to make sure it wasn't a dream. It would be something to tell her friends.

Once downstairs, Cherry stood uncertainly, wondering which was the accepted way to the pool. A door at the far end of the hall opened and a severe-looking woman with iron-grey hair and dressed completely in black appeared. The housekeeper, Cherry surmised—rightly. And straight out of a Dickens novel.

On seeing her, the woman came gliding forward, a polite smile on her somewhat formidable face. '*Si, signorina?* Can I help you? There is something you require?'

Not sure if the housekeeper knew the circumstances, Cherry said quickly, 'Mr Carella said I could use the pool. I'm staying here overnight. My car—'

'*Si, si, signorina.*' It was slightly impatient. 'I know of this. The *signore*—he has informed me of your situation. You have everything you need in your room?'

'Yes—yes, thank you.' Cherry thought the housekeeper fitted in well. She was every bit as intimidating as her indomitable employer. Poor, poor Sophia.

'You please to follow me, *signorina.*' Without further ado the woman turned and retraced her steps, stopping at a door which led into a sunny breakfast room which again had doors leading to the garden. The housekeeper opened a cupboard stocked with massive fluffy beach-towels, taking two and handing them to Cherry as she said, 'The pool, *si?*' She pointed into the distance. 'I will send Gilda or Rosa with the iced drink shortly, *signorina.*'

'Oh, no, please don't go to any trouble on my account,' Cherry said hastily. 'I'll be fine, really.'

'Is no trouble, *signorina.*'

The stern face hadn't mellowed an iota, and feeling as though she was five years old and back in school again, being reprimanded by a teacher for some misdemeanour, Cherry thanked the housekeeper again and stepped out into the hot sunshine.

The quality of light and the intensity of colour she'd noticed since arriving in Italy seemed even more pronounced in the beautiful gardens she walked through to reach the pool. She breathed in the scented air, taking it deep into her lungs. The pool was huge, the water crystalline under the clear blue sky, and on the surrounding tiled area there were several sun-loungers, hammocks and exterior sofas dotted round marble tables—some in the shade of magnolia, oleander and orange trees, and others under parasols. But a number were in the full glare of the sun. It was the perfect place for an afternoon siesta.

Throwing her towels on to a hammock in dappled shade, Cherry slipped off the sarong and walked to the edge of the pool, diving into the deep end without hesitation. The water felt icy to her heated skin, but exhilarating, and she cut through the water with powerful strokes, feeling tinglingly alive. She had always loved swimming since a small child. It was the only sport she had excelled at—unlike Angela, who had been good at everything.

Annoyed with herself that she'd let thoughts of Angela intrude, Cherry cleared her mind of everything but the sensation of the cold water and the heat of the sun above, swimming back and forth at a punishing pace until after ten minutes she was exhausted. Climbing out, she wrapped one of the towels around her middle and positioned the other one in the hammock—just as Rosa appeared with a tray holding a jug of iced fruit juice and a plate of small sugared biscuits.

After thanking the maid she drank a glass of the fruit juice, ate three of the biscuits, and then positioned herself carefully in the hammock, intending to go straight to sleep. Instead she was suddenly reliving the last ugly scene with Angela and Liam, the suddenness of the onslaught taking her completely by surprise. Sitting up so quickly she was almost tipped out on to the hot tiles, she brushed wet hair out of her eyes, angry and upset at her weakness. It was over—done with. You've moved on, she told herself fiercely. You wouldn't have Liam back if he came giftwrapped, so no more dredging up the past.

You're finished with all that—and, anyway, they're not worth it.

'Cherry?' The soft female voice brought her out of the maelstrom of emotion, and as her eyes focused she saw Sophia was standing in front of her, her voluptuous curves accentuated by the scarlet bikini she was wearing. 'Are you unwell?'

Hastily composing her face into a smile, she said, 'No, no, I'm fine. I was just thinking, that's all.'

Sophia sat down on a sun-lounger, a few feet from the hammock. 'Unpleasant thoughts?'

'You could say that.'

'Oh, *scusi*. I do not wish to pry,' Sophia said quickly, clearly taking Cherry's reply as a rebuff.

'No, it's all right.' Cherry felt sorry for this beautiful girl who was a prisoner in her own home. 'I was in love with someone and he dumped me for someone else. It's as simple as that,' she said lightly.

'Is never simple.' Emerald eyes surveyed her compassionately.

'No, you're right. It never is.'

'Do you want to talk about it?'

Surprisingly, Cherry found she did—probably because until this point she hadn't opened up to anyone. She had never been one to wear her heart on her sleeve. All her life the more something hurt her, the more she put on a brave face and carried on. 'I worked with Liam,' she said quietly, 'and we were good friends before we started going out together. I—I thought he was different to most men, that I could trust him implicitly. We'd been together for six months and things were getting serious—talk of engagement and all that—so I thought

I'd better take him home and introduce him to my family.'

'You had not done this before?' Sophia was clearly amazed.

Cherry shook her head. 'My father died a few years ago, and—and I don't get on with my mother and sister.' Understatement of the year, but how could she explain to a virtual stranger how it was? 'My sister saw Liam and wanted him.' She shrugged. 'Within a couple of weeks he told me he'd been seeing her on the nights he didn't see me, and that he'd fallen in love with her.'

'Your sister did not confess?'

'She lives at home with my mother. I live—lived—in a bedsit and we never met up. Angela…' She tried to find the right words. 'She's a year older than me and was always the beautiful, clever one and my mother's favourite. For some reason, even as a child, she always wanted what I had and my mother would insist I gave it to her. Presents, clothes, whatever. Even friends. After I'd escaped to university I never went home to live again.'

'Had your sister done this before? With a boy?'

Cherry nodded. 'That was the reason I didn't introduce Liam to them until I was sure about him.' She shrugged again. 'But it was clearly a mistake.'

'I think not, Cherry.' Sophia leaned forward, her hair rippling like a black curtain. 'This Liam—he was not for you. A man who can behave in such a way—' she flicked her hand, Latin-style, expressing her disgust '—he is weak, no good. Without the backbone, you know? You deserve better.'

'I came to that conclusion a little while ago.' Cherry smiled at Vittorio's sister. 'It took some time, but one day at work I looked at him and didn't like what I saw.

I decided I wanted a change—a real change. So I gave in my notice forthwith, told my landlady I was moving out, and took out all my savings and decided to travel for a bit. Italy is my first port of call, but I intend to see all the Mediterranean and then who knows?' She wrinkled her nose. 'My mother said I was having a tantrum when I rang to tell her what I was doing. She called me ridiculous and impetuous and told me not to ring her if I got into any trouble—not that I would have, of course.'

Sophia shook her head slowly. 'They do not sound nice people, your sister and your mother.'

'No, they're not,' Cherry said candidly, 'but my father was a love. At least I always had an ally in him when I was growing up. He was more than a dad. He was my best friend too.'

'A divided home.' Sophia's voice was soft. 'This is not good. It must have been painful for you.'

Cherry stared at the Italian girl. Vittorio had said his sister had the mind of a sixteen-year-old and had intimated a young sixteen-year-old at that. She didn't agree with him. Sophia was very mature for her years, and very sweet.

The other girl's genuine sympathy and kindness brought sudden tears to her eyes, but Cherry blinked them away determinedly. 'It wasn't the happiest of childhoods,' she admitted quietly, 'but better than some. Some children have no one, do they?'

Sophia nodded. 'I have only a vague memory of my father and mother, but we have the—how you say?—the films. Camera films? Of us as a family before the accident.'

'Home movies.'

'*Si*, home movies. Vittorio, he was born a year after

my parents married, but then there were no more *bambini*. My *madre—scusi*, my mother—was very sad and they saw many doctors. Then when all hope was gone I was born—on Vittorio's twenty-first birthday. Vittorio said the party went on for days, and everyone was very happy.' She beamed at Cherry. 'Vittorio, he says he has never had another present to equal me.'

Cherry smiled. 'I can understand that.'

'But then the accident—a car accident when I was six years old, just before Vittorio was going to be married.' She shrugged. 'Caterina, his fiancée, would not come here to live and so...' She shrugged again. 'Vittorio gave her the house he had bought for them in Matera and after a while Caterina married someone else. I do not like her,' she added, somewhat venomously.

Fascinated by the story, Cherry couldn't resist asking, 'Do you still see Caterina, then?'

'*Si*. She married one of Vittorio's friends. Lorenzo is a nice man. He does not deserve to have such a wife.'

Sophia was certainly a girl who said what she thought. Hiding a smile, Cherry said, 'Didn't Vittorio mind her marrying a friend of his?'

'I do not know. I know they quarrelled because Vittorio would not hand me over to be brought up by our grandmother. He knew my parents would have wanted me to continue to live here under my brother's protection.'

And so he'd sacrificed his own happiness for Sophia. This revelation didn't fit in with her summing up of Vittorio. It was disturbing. Wriggling into a more secure position on the hammock, Cherry said, 'He must love you very much.'

'*Si*. And I love Vittorio. Although he is the most...'

A string of Italian words spoken at great speed followed. Cherry didn't understand one, but she didn't have to to get their meaning.

Eventually Sophia stopped, shaking her head. 'He makes me mad,' she said, an unnecessary statement after what had preceded it. 'He thinks I am still a *bambino*, a child, but I am not. I know what I want and it is not to go to the finishing school he has arranged.'

Cherry thought she probably knew the answer to her next question, but she asked it anyway. 'What *do* you want?'

Sophia flicked her hair over her brown shoulders, her full rounded breasts straining at the thin material holding them as she did so. 'I want to be with Santo. I want to be his wife. But—' she sighed heavily '—Santo is poor. At least compared to us and the families of the girls at school. His family have a small vineyard at the edge of our property and a pretty little farmhouse—*trulli* farmhouse, you understand? They produce the Uva di Troia grape and it is very good. It gives the fine red wine, *si*? But Vittorio has forbidden us to meet.'

'Perhaps he thinks you are too young to think of settling down yet?' She actually agreed with Vittorio on that score, at least. Sophia was sixteen years old; she had years and years in front of her before marriage and all it entailed.

Sophia tossed her head. 'I have known Santo all my life and there will be no one else for either of us. And he is not a young boy. He is nineteen years old this summer.' This was said with an air of proving Santo was as old as Methuselah. 'He is a man. And he is kind, good.' The slightly defiant tone vanished in the next instant. Tears in her eyes, Sophia whispered, 'I would run away and get married, but Santo will not hear of this. If I go to the finishing school I shall not see Santo for a long time and I cannot bear it. I would rather kill myself,' she finished tragically.

'Oh, Sophia.' Cherry slid off the hammock and knelt down beside Vittorio's sister, taking one of her hands. 'If you love each other as much as you say, it will work out in time. I know that's not much comfort now, but you are still young, you know.'

'I do not feel young.' Eyes as green as grass held hers. 'I do not think I have ever truly felt young as my friends are. I have always felt different. And I know what I want, Cherry. I want to marry Santo and have his babies. That is all I have ever wanted. Everything else does not count for me.'

Oh, dear. Somewhat at a loss, Cherry squeezed the slim fingers in hers. 'Then it will happen,' she said simply. 'When it's right. He'll wait for you, if he is the one.'

They talked a little more. Cherry told Vittorio's sister about her job in marketing, and what it had entailed, adding that she was glad she had left when she had and that she was considering a change of career when she returned to England eventually. 'Perhaps local government—something like that. My degree is in English and Business Studies, but I think I'd find social services more interesting. I'm not sure. Time will tell. For now I'm looking on the next few months as the gap year I never had before university.'

Sophia nodded, but clearly had no interest in a career herself, only becoming animated when she told Cherry about Santo and how wonderful he was. 'He has never looked at another girl. I know this,' she said passionately, 'and I could never love anyone else. It is foolish to make us wait. I tell Vittorio this but he will not listen. He has the heart of ice, not of fire.'

After a while both girls settled down for a siesta in the shade of the trees, the chirruping of birds and the lazy hum of bees in the surrounding vegetation the only sound disturbing the warm scented air. Cherry could hardly believe she'd told a virtual stranger about Liam and Angela, but then maybe it was because Sophia *was* a stranger that it had proved so easy. That and these incredibly beautiful and surreal surroundings.

This whole interlude felt like a step out of time, she thought drowsily in the moments before sleep overcame her. It was as though she had been transported to another dimension—a dimension ruled by a dark and autocratic overlord with a heart of stone.

CHAPTER THREE

WHEN Cherry awoke it was because some sixth sense was telling her to beware. From a deep sleep her eyes flew open, and she raised her head to stare into the beautiful smoky-grey eyes that had featured in a dream she now couldn't remember but which she knew had been disturbing.

'Sleeping Beauty.' Vittorio's voice was soft and deep. 'This is a fairytale, *si*?'

It might be—but never had the Prince been dressed in nothing but a brief pair of swimming trunks, and she didn't think even Prince Charming's body could compete with the man in front of her. The flagrant masculinity had been raw enough when Vittorio had been fully dressed. Now it was positively alarming. His thickly muscled torso gleamed like oiled silk, and he had obviously just been in the pool because the tight black curls on his chest glistened with droplets of water. The hair on his chest narrowed to a thin line over his flat belly, disappearing into the trunks, and his thighs were hard and powerful. He looked lean, lithe and dangerous, and undeniably earth-shattering.

Cherry swallowed. There was something about Vittorio Carella which made her feel completely subjugated and painfully feminine. She could cope with the second emotion, but the first was causing her hackles to rise again. Nevertheless, she did what she'd promised herself she would do the next time she saw him and said quickly, 'I must apologise for not thanking you properly for allowing me to stay. I'm not usually so rude.'

He eyed her speculatively for a moment, then stretched out on the sun-lounger his sister had used earlier. Lazily, he drawled, 'Then why so remiss today, Cherry?'

She might have known she couldn't expect him simply to accept her apology and leave it at that. It took all of her considerable willpower to bite back the tart retort hovering on her tongue and say flatly, 'Probably because we got off on the wrong foot.'

'The wrong foot?' He was clearly amused. 'This is an English expression, *si*? But why did we get off on this "wrong foot", eh? I think I know the answer to this.'

She stared at him, not knowing what to say.

'For some reason you do not like me. This is true, *si*?'

She could tell he was enjoying her discomfiture, playing with her like a cat with a mouse, and nothing could have stopped her next words. 'As it happens, you're dead right.' So much for the apology. But it was his fault, not hers.

'You are an independent woman, I think. Strong. And surprisingly unmaterialistic.'

She didn't know if she agreed with his opinion— certainly with regard to the first two attributes. She hadn't felt very strong lately. Weakly, she said, 'Surprisingly?'

'I have found most modern women are driven by avarice and greed when it comes to looking for a partner in the opposite sex.'

Cherry reared up like a scalded cat, glaring at him with shocked eyes. 'That's absolutely ridiculous.'

'You think so?' He smiled coldly. 'But this is not a criticism, Cherry. Most mothers want their daughters to marry well and live a life of luxury. It is natural. And most daughters are only too pleased to be guided by Mamma in this respect. Over the last years I have had a whole host of such daughters paraded before me by hopeful matrons who probably know to the last euro what I am worth. And of course there have been other women—socialites and so on—who thought they would like to become Signora Carella and continue to live in the manner to which they were accustomed. A few have even said this outright.'

She stared at him. 'Are you saying women only want you for your money?' Had he looked in the mirror lately?

He laughed—a throaty chuckle. 'Not *only* my money, no. If there was a choice between a rich old man and a rich young one most red-blooded females would prefer the latter, I have no doubt. But wealth and position are powerful aphrodisiacs.'

Cherry thought he was doing himself—and probably the vast majority of the women he'd spoken of—a grave injustice. Vittorio Carella was the epitome of a man with everything, and she didn't doubt women would find it easy to fall in love with him. She found the thought uncomfortable, and because of this her voice was uncharacteristically sharp when she said, 'Something tells me you have been mixing with the wrong type of woman. Or maybe it's a case of "live by the sword, die by the sword"?'

'An interesting suggestion.' His voice was smooth, silky, but there was the slightest of inflexion in the cool foreign voice that hinted he wasn't as relaxed and non-chalant as he'd have her believe. 'You are intimating I get what I deserve, *signorina*?'

'My father always used to say that water finds its own level.' She smiled, determined not to be intimidated by this arrogant individual who had put womankind into a box. 'And I happen to have lots of female friends who couldn't care less about the balance of a man's bank account but put a high price on faithfulness and commitment.'

'And you, Cherry? Do you put a high price on faithfulness?'

For a second she wondered if Sophia had told him about Liam and Angela, but almost immediately dismissed the thought. Brother and sister weren't into cosy conversations just at the moment. She took a deep breath and spoke from the heart. 'It's priceless.'

The grey eyes narrowed before he raked back his wet hair with bronzed fingers. Changing the subject with an abruptness which was unnerving, he said, 'I saw Sophia talking to you earlier.' He gestured towards the house. 'From the window. The conversation appeared...intense.'

Cherry's chin tilted upwards. To anyone who knew her it was a warning signal, but her voice was controlled and without heat when she said calmly, 'I have no intention of repeating my conversation with your sister, Signor Carella.'

'I didn't think you would, Miss Cherry Gibbs from England. Not for a moment. You think Sophia is hard done by?'

The overt mockery was galling. *He* was galling, with his to-die-for body and filmstar good-looks. Horrified such a thought had entered her mind, Cherry said crisply,

'I would just say that I consider your treatment of your sister archaic at best and stupid at worst.'

The smile hovering about his mouth disappeared. 'Stupid?' he ground out. Clearly 'archaic' was permissible, but 'stupid' had most definitely touched a nerve.

He sat up on the sun-bed, the subtle sensual odour of his brown skin overlaid with the tang of the swimming-pool water filling her senses as he leant closer. 'Why stupid?' he murmured, his eyes like cold steel. 'Explain yourself.'

He *had* asked. 'I happen to think Sophia is far more emotionally mature than you intimated,' she said carefully, 'but when all is said and done she is still a sixteen-year-old girl. I've been that age, and if there is one thing absolutely set in concrete it's that you do whatever the older generation says it's foolish to do. Call it rebellion, finding your own feet, whatever, but it's guaranteed you'll go against the grain. And that is what Sophia is doing.'

'Santo?' he said flatly.

'Santo.' Cherry nodded. 'You are driving her into his arms by trying to keep them apart.'

'The *problema romantico*?' The hard, autocratic face was thoughtful. '*Si*, maybe. Perhaps you have a point.'

'Yes, definitely.' Her voice was cool. 'It's Romeo and Juliet all over again.'

'An exaggeration, but I get your drift,' he drawled mockingly.

Hateful man. 'Of course it's none of my business,' she said crisply, sliding out of the hammock and walking towards the swimming pool. 'And I'm sure a man as well acquainted with the female sex as you obviously are knows exactly what he's doing.'

She dived into the cool water before he could reply, needing to put some space between them. It didn't work. When she surfaced he was right there beside her, grey eyes glinting in the baking hot sunlight.

He didn't mince his words. 'You think I am a womaniser?' he asked, treading water by her side. 'A philanderer?'

Feeling far more vulnerable than she would have liked, Cherry blinked and shook her hair out of her eyes. 'I've no idea what you are,' she prevaricated. 'I don't know you, do I?'

'This is true, but I do not think it has stopped you forming an opinion.' As she began to swim, he kept by her side. 'Are you always so quick to make erroneous judgements?'

His voice was mild, but it didn't fool her for a moment. She had got under his skin, it was obvious, but any satisfaction she might have felt about denting his giant ego was negated by a feeling of defencelessness. Not that she thought he would hurt her—she didn't—but...

Forcing a calmness into her voice that was all at odds with her wildly beating heart, she said, 'I told you. I have no opinion about you one way or the other, OK? You might have a woman for every day of the week or you could live like a monk. You were the one who talked about all those daughters of marriagable age being paraded before you, remember?'

They had reached the shallow end of the pool, where large circular steps led gently into the water. Cherry didn't know whether to climb out or continue swimming, but in the next moment Vittorio murmured, 'Ah, here is Margherita. I thought it would be nice to have cocktails by the pool tonight before dinner.'

He seriously expected her to sit half-naked drinking cocktails with him? Worse, the scrap of material posing as swimming trunks which all Italian men seemed to favour left nothing, absolutely nothing, to the imagination. The water was cold but Cherry felt hot all over as she watched the housekeeper's approach.

Would she be reacting differently to his intimidating masculinity if she'd gone to bed with a man before? she asked herself feverishly as Vittorio stood up, offering his hand to her as he stood on the bottom step leading out of the pool. Possibly because she knew Angela had always slept around, even having two or three boyfriends on the go now and again, Cherry had always determined she would wait for 'the one' before she gave herself body and soul. She supposed in hindsight it said a lot for her lack of confidence that she and Liam would actually last, that she hadn't given in to his constant demands that their lovemaking progress beyond the petting stage. Introducing him to Angela had been the big test. And he'd failed. Spectacularly. But had it really been a surprise?

Realising she couldn't do anything other than take Vittorio's hand, she, too, stood up, blessing the fact she was wearing her chaste swimming costume, its colour and cut modest. What she didn't comprehend was that when the material was wet it clung to her body like a second skin, showing every dip and curve in a way more skimpy bikinis couldn't hope to achieve. And then she glanced at Vittorio and saw the blazing animal desire turning the grey eyes into hot glittering orbs, before his lids came down and hid their expression from her.

Shocked, she stumbled on the slippery steps, and but for his fingers tightening round hers she would have fallen.

'Come.' His voice was cool and controlled as he led her out of the water, letting go of her hand immediately once she was standing safely on the hot marble slabs surrounding the pool area and turning to the housekeeper who was waiting for them. '*Grazie*, Margherita,' he said, taking the tray holding two large fluted cocktail glasses and little bowls of nuts and other nibbles from the other woman. 'Sophia is not joining us?'

The housekeeper answered in Italian, and whatever she said caused Vittorio to shrug. 'Then we will see her at dinner. You will make this clear to her. I will have no more sulking in her room, pleading she is feeling unwell. Not now we have a guest.'

'Oh, please, don't make her come and eat dinner on my account,' Cherry said hastily, wondering how quickly she could get to her sarong and cover herself. She had never felt so embarrassed in her life. Why hadn't she realised before how positively indecent the swimming costume became when wet? But then Vittorio Carella hadn't been around before.

Vittorio ignored her as though she hadn't spoken. 'You will make it clear,' he repeated to his housekeeper, who stood stiff and impassive in the golden sunshine like a large black crow. Glancing at Cherry, whose cheeks were scarlet, he nodded in the direction of the hammock and sun-lounger they'd vacated. 'Shall we?'

He let her precede him, and it was the hardest thing she'd ever done to walk in front of him. She knew his eyes were on her bottom, she could feel their heat burning into her skin, but it was better than if he was facing her because the air on her wet costume had turned her nipples into hard peaks pressing against the thin fabric. She felt as though she was in a porn movie.

It seemed like for ever before she reached the hammock and grabbed the sarong, wrapping it round her and tying it firmly over the top of her breasts so she was covered to her knees.

Vittorio set the tray on a table next to his sun-lounger, his voice lazy when he murmured, 'Better?' and glanced at her.

Her colour had just begun to subside. Now it flared into brighter life again at the knowledge he'd sensed her embarrassment and the reason for it. 'I'm sorry?' she said icily.

'You are feeling better now you are out of the glare of the sun and under the shade of the trees?' he drawled softly. 'The English skin is sensitive, *si*? It burns easily.'

It wasn't what he had meant, and he knew that she knew it. She could tell from the wicked amusement in his eyes. Struggling for composure, she told herself not to rise to his bait. 'I've been in Italy for a few days now. My skin is beginning to acclimatise. Besides which I'm fortunate in that I go brown very easily and rarely burn.'

'This is good.' He patted the sun-lounger next to his. 'Come and enjoy your cocktail and relax before you change for dinner.'

Relaxing *so* wasn't an option. Not with acres of hard male flesh causing difficulty with her breathing. And Vittorio was so very much at ease with his body, which didn't help. He made her feel gauche in the extreme. No doubt the women he'd spoken of earlier would have been quite in command of themselves and the situation, and more than willing to flaunt themselves.

Somehow she found the aplomb to walk over to the sun-lounger and sit down with a certain grace, a polite smile on her face as she accepted the cocktail he handed her. In any other circumstances, with any other man, she would be enjoying this brief interlude out of real life, she thought regretfully, as she took a sip of her drink.

'Wow!' As the cocktail hit her tastebuds she gasped. 'Whatever's this?' It was delicious but lethal.

'It is called "Love in the Afternoon",' said Vittorio, deadpan. 'Do you like it?'

She stared at him suspiciously. 'Is it really called that?'

'But of course.' He smiled. 'It is one of my own concoctions for lazy summer afternoons like this one.'

That explained it. She'd dare bet he never sat here drinking it by himself! She had to swallow hard before she said primly, 'It's very nice, but it tastes rather potent.'

One male eyebrow slanted provocatively. 'As one would expect, surely?'

He smiled that sexy smile but she refused to respond.

His shoulders were muscled and wide. He was muscled all over, but without an inch of fat on his lean frame. He hadn't moved since passing her the cocktail, but ridiculously Cherry felt she wanted to edge away. She didn't of course.

Clearing her throat, she took another tentative sip. 'What's in it?'

'Gin, dry orange curacao liqueur, chilled champagne, fresh lime juice and pressed pineapple. Little more than a fruit punch, really,' he said gently.

A fruit punch guaranteed to do exactly what the name suggested after a glass or two, she'd be bound. Cherry eyed him severely. 'Hardly your average fruit punch. In England—'

'Ah, but you are not in England now, are you, *mia piccola*?' he murmured. 'England is such a cold country, I have found. Even your summers are full of rain and chilly winds, and you need the fire to keep you warm. I have no doubt your English punch lacks the passion and heat of Italy.'

He made it sound as though everyone and everything in England was as cold as ice, and she had no doubt he was having a none too subtle dig at her. She knew she ought to leave it, but somehow she couldn't. 'I can assure you English people are just as impassioned as Italians about things that matter,' she said tightly. 'Admittedly we don't wear our hearts on our sleeves all the time, but that doesn't mean we don't feel deeply.'

'I thought we were talking about punch?'

'Punch and other things.'

His frown smoothed to a quizzical ruffle. 'I see. So, while we are on the subject, are *you* passionate about things that matter, Cherry? And, if so, what makes your heart beat faster?'

She took a long sip of her drink, needing its boost. 'All sorts of things.' She eyed him warily.

He swung his legs on to the floor, finishing his cocktail in a couple of gulps and putting the glass on the tray before he sat studying her with unnerving concentration. 'Name one.'

His change of position had brought him so close she felt enveloped by his body warmth even though he wasn't touching her. He was so near that she could see the tiny black hairs under his skin on the hard jawline, the amazing thickness of his long lashes. He had the most beautiful mouth, she thought dazedly. Firm, strong, sensual.

Blaming the thought on the cocktail, she made a Herculean effort to pull herself together. 'I love animals,' she said weakly. 'Reading, eating out with friends—'

He interrupted her with scathing abruptness. 'I did

not ask for the sort of details you put on a CV. I asked about the real you.'

She glared at him. 'That is the real me.' Part of the real her anyway. The only bit she was prepared to share with him.

'And what about love? Romance? Is there anyone special at home in your cold England? A sweetheart waiting for you?'

She wasn't aware of the stiffening of her expression, the blink of her eyes, the slight lift of her chin, but the piercing grey gaze took in every nuance of her body language. 'No.' It was too abrupt and she realised it immediately, adding in what she sincerely hoped was a light voice, 'Not at the moment.'

'But there was until recently? Is that why you came to Italy? To escape from him?'

Anger provided a welcome shot of adrenaline. Cherry's glare magnified until her blue eyes flashed sparks. 'I don't think that is any of your business, but as it happens there was no "escape" about it. I have chosen to take a few months exploring the continent at a time when I am footloose and fancy-free, without any ties. It's really very straightforward.'

'You have not answered my question,' he said gently.

Cherry plonked her glass on the low table at the side of her, spilling some of the cocktail, and stood up. 'I'm very grateful for your hospitality,' she said icily, her face burning, 'but, like I said, my personal life is absolutely none of your business.'

He'd risen too, and without a word took her into his arms and kissed her. It was a warm, experimental kiss at first, and she was so taken aback she let it happen. By the time it deepened into an invasive probing she couldn't have moved if she'd wanted to. His touch had fired a hundred tingling signals to her senses. It was the sort of kiss she'd dreamed of as an adolescent, sweet and hot.

He placed a hand in the small of her back to steady her, drawing her closer into his lean frame until she was moulded to the hard planes of his body. The rough magic of his body hair teased her silky-smooth skin as his mouth fuelled the rush of sensation his lips and tongue were producing, tiny sharp needles of pleasure injecting desire into her veins like a forbidden drug.

'Delicious…' he murmured softly against her lips as the deliberate assault on her senses continued, the mouth she had thought so beautiful sensuously coaxing.

The warm fragrant air, the shadows of light and dark against her closed eyelids, the ache in the core of her all contributed to the feeling of dreamlike unrealness that had taken Cherry over. The last months had been hard and painful and humiliating, and this fantasy interlude was all the more seductive because of it. She felt desirable, womanly, and it was heady.

She shifted in his arms, but only so that she could lift her hands to his broad shoulders, abandoning herself to his lovemaking with an eagerness that would have shocked her if she had been capable of rational thought. But she didn't want to think. She'd done enough thinking since the moment she'd learned Liam had betrayed her to last a lifetime. She just wanted to *be*…

Vittorio's thighs were hard against her soft curves as the hand on her back slid lower, moving her hips forward to fit her body into his. And it was this, the unmistakable feel of his hot arousal, that jerked Cherry back into sanity. Her hands pushed at his chest as she wrenched herself free, taking a step backwards, and her breath was a sob as she whispered, 'Don't. I don't want this.'

He made no attempt to reach for her again. He was breathing hard and took a moment to compose himself before he spoke. His voice was dry. 'Finish your cocktail, *mia piccola*,' he murmured, 'while I take the equivalent of a cold shower.' And with that he turned, walked swiftly to the edge of the pool, and dived into its cool depths.

CHAPTER FOUR

CHERRY didn't even wait for Vittorio to surface before she grabbed her glass and dashed back towards the house. The gardens were slumbering in the early evening sunshine, and the heat of the day was still making itself felt, but she covered the distance quicker than an Olympic athlete, terrified he might call to her. And she couldn't bear to face him right now.

She dived into the breakfast room and then out into the hall, skidding on the marble floor and almost ending up in one of the exquisite flower displays, before running up the stairs. It wasn't until she had entered her room and shut the door, locking it for good measure, that she realised she was still holding her now empty glass.

Sinking down on to the bed, she placed the glass carefully on the bedside cabinet before putting her hands over her hot face. What an exhibition she'd made of herself— not only allowing him to kiss her like that but then bolting away like a scared little rabbit. She should have stayed and finished the cocktail, greeting him coolly when he returned with some casual, offhand remark to defuse any embarrassment. She groaned softly.

Not that he'd been embarrassed. She shut her eyes, but she could still see the hard inches of male arousal straining against the material of his swimming trunks—proof that he had wanted her, right then and there. His face had shown it too, sexual knowledge turning the grey eyes hungry with anticipation. He'd clearly thought from her response to him that he was on to a good thing. She groaned again, burning with shame. And then she had pushed him away like a frightened schoolgirl and further compounded her stupidity by sprinting for the house as though the devil was after her. What on earth had she looked like?

He'd think she was a tease—one of those women who indicated she was available and ready for the taking and then backed off at the last moment. She pressed a fist to her mouth to stop herself groaning for a third time.

And how could she explain otherwise? How could she say his kiss had been the most mind-blowing experience of her life? He'd either think she was playing sexual games or, worse, that she fancied him and was trying to reel him in. Give a wolf a taste and keep him hungry. Either way it was back to the tease thing again. And she had never behaved like that in her life. She'd heard other girls—at university and later in the workplace—discuss strategies to keep a man dangling, and such manipulation disgusted her. But Vittorio wasn't to know that.

Cherry sat for another few minutes, heaping self-denigration on herself, before walking into the bathroom. A bath. A long soak in bubbles. This was one occasion when a shower wouldn't do. She would wash her hair and cream and pamper herself, perhaps even paint her nails with one of the bottles of varnish she'd seen earlier, and when she went downstairs for dinner she would be in full command of herself.

Her stomach cringed at the thought of facing Vittorio,

but she stared at her tragic face in the mirror and almost smiled. Why he'd wanted to kiss her in the first place she'd never know. She looked like a little waif and stray the wind had blown in. All eyes and trembling lips. But no more. She hadn't brought much with her in the way of evening clothes—it wasn't that sort of holiday—but she did have a couple of dresses that had cost an arm and a leg. She had bought them in the aftermath of the split with Liam, when she'd been feeling ugly and worthless, and they'd been worth every penny for the confidence they'd given her. One of those would do just fine. The deep blue viscose-crêpe one with the asymmetric lace border, perhaps. She had a pair of leather strappy sandals which would set off the cut of the dress. And she'd put her hair up. It made her look older.

An hour later she was just teasing a few silky strands from the large clip shed used to put her hair up when there was a knock at the bedroom door. Her heart somersaulted and then beat so hard she couldn't breathe. Somehow she managed to say, 'Yes? Who is it?' and the relief when Sophia's voice came a moment later was immense. She'd thought… And then she shook her head at her own fancifulness. Why would a man like Vittorio bother with her anyway? He had plenty more fish in the sea, no doubt.

When she opened the door, Sophia smiled at her. Vittorio's sister looked even older in the green strapless dress she was wearing, her voluptuous hour-glass figure perfectly suited to the deceptively simple A-line evening frock. 'I thought we could go down together, Cherry.'

'Yes, of course. I just need to find my sandals.' Cherry opened the door wider and Sophia came in, shutting it behind her. Cherry knelt down by her open case on the floor, digging inside for the sandals—the only dressy shoes she'd brought with her. Once she had fished them out she sat back on her heels with them in her hands. 'Sorry to keep you waiting,' she began, turning her head, and then, her voice changing as she saw tears running down Sophia's face, she said, 'Oh, what is it? What's the matter?'

She jumped up, pulling Sophia over to the bed and sitting down with her as she took the younger girl's hands in hers. 'Is it Santo?' she said softly, thinking Vittorio's sister was suddenly overcome by the situation. She was only sixteen, after all, and emotion were hard to control at that age.

'*Si, si*—in a way,' Sophia whispered, seeming quite different from the controlled young woman at the pool that afternoon. 'I—I am in trouble, Cherry, and I have no one to speak to, to confide in. I am so frightened. At the pool—' she sniffed and rubbed at her nose in a childish gesture '—you seemed to understand how I was feeling. But—but there is more.'

Hoping the thought which had immediately sprung to mind was way off beam, Cherry said gently, 'Can't you talk to Vittorio? He does love you, you know, even if he is a little over-protective. He feels responsible for you since your parents died and wants to do the right thing.'

'Vittorio is the last person I can talk to about this.'

Oh, dear. When Sophia seemed unable to go on, Cherry took the plunge. 'Are you pregnant, Sophia?'

Vittorio's sister shut her eyes and then nodded, tears seeping from under her closed lids. 'But it wasn't Santo's fault. Not that Vittorio will believe that. I—I knew what I was doing. He wanted to stop but I needed to belong to him, properly. I wouldn't let him push me away like he'd done before when things went too far. He was beside himself afterwards.'

'And you? What were you like?' Cherry pressed quietly.

Sophia opened her eyes, and although they were swimming with tears her voice was strong when she said, 'I was glad. I still am. Although I didn't expect… I didn't think you could become pregnant the first time.'

Sophia had probably had a first-class education, but Cherry dared bet the young Italian girl had little idea of the birds and the bees. Or had had before. She was certainly more well acquainted with that side of things now, Cherry thought ruefully. Sophia had been so protected all her life, so carefully brought up, and perhaps in her culture such privileged young women were virgins on their wedding night, with only a basic knowledge of birth control and so on. Of course Sophia hadn't had a mother to explain things, and as Vittorio still considered his sister as little more than a child…

What a muddle. Cherry passed Sophia a tissue. 'And Santo? What does he say about this?'

Fresh tears welled up. 'I haven't told him yet. I wasn't absolutely sure, but today when I was shopping with Margherita I pretended I wanted a lipstick from the chemist and bought a kit. You know—it tells you if you're expecting a baby or not. After I'd talked to you by the pool I worked up the courage to do it.' She gazed at Cherry helplessly.

'So there's no doubt?'

Sophia shook her head. 'I've—I've missed two periods now. But I know as soon as I tell Santo he'll come and see Vittorio and say he wants to marry me, and I'm so afraid of what Vittorio will do to him.'

And with good cause, Cherry thought grimly. She had only known Vittorio for a matter of hours, but she wouldn't want to be in Santo's shoes for all the tea in China. 'You have to tell Vittorio, Sophia. You know that, don't you? From all you've told me about Santo he isn't the type to elope or suggest you disappear somewhere with him. He'll come and see Vittorio, and it's important your brother is told the full facts by you first. It will give him a chance to calm down.'

'I cannot, Cherry.' Real fear crossed Sophia's pretty face. She said something in Italian and then, realising Cherry didn't understand, said quickly, 'He has the temper, *si*?'

'But Vittorio has to know, Sophia.' Cherry stared at the Italian girl helplessly. 'You see that, surely?'

'Would you tell my brother, Cherry?' Sophia grabbed Cherry's hands. '*Per favore*? Would you?'

'Me?' Cherry recoiled in horror.

'*Si*. You are a guest in our home. Vittorio will respect this. But me...' Sophia rolled her eyes. 'I dare not.'

'You don't think your brother would harm you?' Cherry said gently. Somehow she was sure Vittorio wouldn't hurt Sophia.

'*Si*. No.' Sophia shook her head, confused. 'I do not know. But if you tell him he will not lose his temper for sure. I know it is asking much, but I beg you.'

It *was* asking much—even without Vittorio's apparent temper to contend with. She had only known them both a matter of hours.

'We love each other, Cherry,' Sophia said earnestly. 'We always have. And I can move into the farmhouse with Santo's family once we are married. Santo has a room all to himself. It will not be a problem. And his parents like me. His *madre*—his mother—she is so sweet. Santo can continue working with his father, and I can help his mother in the house. I will be company for her. Santo has five sisters, but they are older than him and married with their own homes.'

Sophia had it all worked out. Cherry stared at the other girl. *Had* she fallen pregnant by accident, or was she not quite as ingenuous as she claimed? Whatever, the deed was done. A baby was on the way—the true innocent in this tangle—and was to be born to a couple who were little more than children themselves. But from what Sophia had said she and Santo would not be coping with a newborn by themselves, like some young people. With grandparents on hand, their lot would be easier.

'Now you are sure you're expecting a baby, you need to tell Santo, Sophia. He has a right to know before anyone else.' Cherry stood up. 'He is the father after all.'

'*Si*. You are right.' Sophia stood up too. 'And if I do this will you tell Vittorio?'

Cherry felt she was between the devil and the deep blue sea—the devil definitely being Vittorio, she thought wryly. But in one way she could follow Sophia's reasoning that the news coming from a stranger might keep the lid on Vittorio's rage, and by the time he saw Sophia he might have calmed down a little. Two mights. Two too many, considering she was going to be in the firing line. 'I'm leaving tomorrow once the car is delivered,' she warned Sophia.

'*Si*, but there is after dinner tonight, or maybe breakfast? Perhaps tonight is better, in case the car comes early, and Vittorio will be more relaxed, more mellow, having eaten dinner and drunk wine. I can disappear early, before coffee. I will say I have the headache. I can slip out while Margherita is seeing to things in the kitchen and tell Santo. Then we come back to face Vittorio together. This is good, eh?' Sophia smiled hopefully. 'And you can tell him it is not Santo's fault.'

Oh, hell. And all because some ne'er do well had syphoned off her petrol. She should be installed in a nice little *pensioni* up the coast by now, with nothing more important on her mind than what she was going to have for dinner. The last thing she wanted was to be embroiled in a situation like this, when it could well be a case of 'shoot the messenger'. Flatly, she said, 'What would you have done if I hadn't turned up today?'

Sophia shrugged and then smiled again. 'But you did, and I will always be glad of it,' she said disarmingly. 'I have been praying to Our Lady since I suspected I might be expecting a baby, asking her to help me, and now she has.'

It brought home to Cherry how very young Sophia was, in spite of her womanly appearance. She couldn't let Sophia face her brother alone. Sighing, she said, 'After dinner, then.'

'Grazie, grazie.' Sophia flung her arms round Cherry and hugged her. 'I wish you could stay for a while and see me married. I have always wanted a sister.'

'You're going to acquire five shortly,' Cherry said drily.

Sophia giggled, all tears gone. 'This is true, and they have many *bambini*. My little one, he will not be lonely.'

Feeling things were again verging on the surreal, Cherry slipped on her sandals. Sophia had gone from desperation to delight in a couple of minutes, and she couldn't help feeling Vittorio's sister hadn't embraced the enormity of the changes which were inevitably going to occur in her life. She just hoped the wonderful Santo came up to scratch tonight. Sophia didn't have a shred of doubt in her mind that he would offer to marry her.

They walked downstairs together, and once in the hall Sophia led the way into the drawing room where Vittorio was sitting with a drink. Sophia's revelation had driven the events of the afternoon out of Cherry's mind, but now all she could see was Vittorio as he'd been by the pool—practically naked and hugely aroused. Two spots of blazing colour stained her cheekbones as she met the cool grey eyes.

'Every man's dream,' he murmured lazily, 'to dine with *two* beautiful women. Come and have a drink.'

Somehow Cherry's legs carried her across the room to sit beside Sophia on one of the sofas. Vittorio was wearing beautifully cut black trousers and a snow-white shirt open at the throat, and he looked sensational. He was the kind of man it was difficult to imagine had once been a small boy, but no doubt he'd had every little girl for miles around madly in love with him. When they'd been handing out sex appeal Vittorio must have stood in line twice. And then some.

'Another cocktail, Cherry?' he asked silkily. 'I think you spilt most of the one by the pool. Or perhaps you would prefer wine or a sherry?'

So he had noticed her ignominious flight earlier. And of course he had to let her know. Cherry's chin came up, and in spite of her pink cheeks her voice was as thin as steel as she said, 'I don't care for cocktails. Wine would be fine.' She nodded to the open bottle on the coffee table in front of him. 'Whatever you're having.'

He bent forward and poured a good measure of the deep red wine into one of the two waiting glasses, handing it to her before filling the other glass with an equal measure of wine and lemonade which he passed to Sophia. His sister grimaced. 'For goodness' sake, I am nearly seventeen, Vittorio. When are you going to start treating me as an adult rather than a child?'

Ignoring Sophia, he smiled at Cherry. 'You have everything you need in your room?'

She had just taken a sip of the wine and almost choked as the grey gaze fastened on her, swallowing hard before she said, 'Yes, thank you,' with studied politeness.

He nodded, settling back in his chair and stretching his long legs in front of him. She had caught a whiff of clean, sharp aftershave as he'd handed her the wine, and now his maleness seemed to cross the space between them and surround her, making it difficult to breathe.

She was unutterably glad when Margherita appeared in the doorway in the next moment, the housekeeper's face impassive when she said, 'Dinner is ready, Signor Carella.'

'Thank you, Margherita. We'll bring our drinks through.'

The dining room was as gorgeous as the rest of the house; an enormous table in exquisite multi-coloured Indian wood was a thing of beauty all by itself, and complemented by the colour scheme of pale buttery yellow and warm ochre which gave an air of tranquillity to the surroundings. The lighting was subdued, the soft muslin drapes at the open windows were moving gently in the warm evening breeze, and the bowl of freshly cut roses in the centre of the table perfumed the air with their sweetness. In any other circumstances it would have been a magical place to sit and chat and savour food and wine. As it was, Cherry's nerves were stretched as tight as piano wire.

Rosa and Gilda appeared with the first course—
antipasto, which consisted of a small plate of olives, cold
meats and anchovies—standing behind Vittorio, who was
seated at the head of the table while he gave thanks for the
meal, and then serving the food quickly and efficiently.

Sophia tucked in with gusto. Apparently the events
which were going to unfold in a few short hours hadn't
affected her appetite, Cherry thought wryly. She glanced
at Vittorio, who was still blissfully unaware of the bomb
about to be dropped in his orderly, controlled world, and
found his eyes were waiting for her. Her stomach flut-
tered nervously.

'Eat,' he said softly, 'or Margherita will think you
do not appreciate her food, which would be taken as a
great insult.'

Before Sophia had come into her room she had been
feeling quite hungry. Now it was an effort to pick up her
cutlery. Nevertheless, once she began eating she found
the food delicious, the sharp contrasts in taste awaken-
ing her tastebuds.

The next course was soup with little shapes of pasta in
it which Vittorio informed her were *orecchiette*. 'Little
ears, in English,' he said with a smile. 'Puglia is a rich
agricultural landscape, as I am sure you have noticed,
and as such the local produce provides a cuisine which
is among the best in Italy. The abundant wheatfields and
the closeness of the coast mean we feast well; food is very
important to us. Is this not right, Sophia?' he added, including his sister in the conversation.

Sophia nodded. 'Try some of Margherita's bread,
Cherry,' she offered, passing the basket to her. 'She
makes it with black olives, onions and tomato, and our
own olive oil.'

The bread was mouth-wateringly good. The best she'd tasted.

At this point in the meal Cherry made up her mind to forget about what was to come and enjoy her dinner. Margherita was clearly a fantastic cook, the wine was like nectar from the gods, and Vittorio had apparently decided to put the incident by the pool behind him and metamorphosed into the perfect host, amusing and attentive, with a dry wit that had her spluttering into her glass more than once.

The condemned man—or in this case woman—ate a hearty meal, Cherry told herself, as she gazed with delight at the main course of *carpaccio*—paper-thin slices of fillet steak garnished with fresh egg mayonnaise and finely slivered Parmesan. It tasted as good as it looked. She thought she had eaten well since she had arrived in Italy, but nothing measured up to Margherita's cooking. Scary she might be, but hey, so what?

'You eat like an Italian.' Vittorio's voice was soft and his voice had a rich smoky tinge to it as he held her eyes, which made her shiver inside.

To combat her reaction to him, she made her voice light when she said, 'I take it that is a good thing?'

'Of course. Italians know how to enjoy the good things in life, *si*? Life is a gift and not to be wasted. Not even for a moment. There are many pleasures to keep the heart glad, and some are even free.'

His eyes danced, and Cherry just knew he was thinking of their kiss, but this time she refused to blush. Doggedly, she said, 'Food has to be paid for, surely?'

'*Si*, this is true. But a lovely sunset, the feel of cold water on hot skin, walking on a deserted beach at the start of a new day, looking at a beautiful woman—these things are free, are they not? And there are many more.'

'Try telling that to the millions of people who live out their lives in concrete jungles called cities with maybe a couple of weeks' holiday somewhere hot.'

She hadn't intended to be confrontational, but somehow it had come out that way. Now it had, though, she didn't intend to apologise, and she looked at Vittorio defiantly.

Vittorio looked back from under his long thick eyelashes. She couldn't read a thing in his inscrutable expression, and had no idea if she'd offended him or not, but forced herself to look back calmly.

'Rome is a city, but I would not call it a concrete jungle,' he said gently. 'Nor Paris, not even London. There are many fine buildings in your capital—squares, parks, places of interest and beauty. Of course there will always be ghettos in every country. It is unfortunate, but while man's greed triumphs over poverty this will be so. Many governments are infected with the virus of dishonesty, and power corrupts, but still the human spirit can find release if it chooses to.'

She stared at him. Not only had the conversation suddenly become very serious, but she felt she'd been well and truly put in her place by an expert. Which maybe she should have expected.

Sophia must have thought so too, and clearly didn't intend to stay around for an argument to develop. She stood up, dropping her linen napkin on the table as she said, 'I have the headache, Vittorio. I think I will go to bed. I am sorry, Cherry, but I shall see you at breakfast, *si*?'

Aware Vittorio's sister was trying to deflect an altercation purely because she didn't want anything to spoil her plans, Cherry forced a smile. 'Yes, of course.' They both knew she was going to see Sophia before that, if Santo reacted as Sophia expected and came to the house to speak to Vittorio.

'You are not staying for dessert?' There was a note of amazement in Vittorio's voice. It was clear his sister had a sweet tooth. 'It is your favourite.'

'No. *Buonanotte*, Cherry.' Sophia walked behind Vittorio's chair, ostensibly to kiss her brother on the cheek but at the same time giving Cherry a meaningful look. '*Buonanotte*, Vittorio.' And with that she made a hurried escape.

As Sophia left the room the two maids bustled in to remove the dirty dishes and serve dessert. This consisted of caramel oranges and home-made ice cream, along with a plate of cheeses including two local ones—*canestrato pugliese*, a hard sheeps' milk cheese, and *burrata*, a creamy cheese within a cheese, surrounded by a 'skin' of mozzarella—both of which Cherry had tried before and liked. But suddenly she couldn't eat another thing. It had been one thing to agree to Sophia's pleading that she break the news to Vittorio in the safety of her bedroom, quite another with Vittorio in front of her. Her heart seemed to want to leap out of her body, and she was glad she was sitting down as her legs had turned to jelly.

'Have I grown horns?' he murmured softly.

'What?' Too late she realised she was staring at him. Hastily she tried to school her features into a more acceptable expression. Not the best start to a difficult conversation.

'Just because Sophia has left the room, I am not about to leap on you and have my wicked way.' He smiled, but it didn't reach the slate-grey eyes. 'You are quite safe, *mia piccola*.'

Shocked, she gathered her wits. 'I know that,' she said tightly. 'I was just thinking, that's all.'

'Of that I have no doubt, but I think it wise not to enquire further. I have the feeling my ego would be more bruised than it is already.' He waved a bronzed hand at her dish of caramel oranges and ice cream. 'Eat your dessert. Margherita will be bringing coffee shortly, and then you can run away again.'

It was the 'again' that did it. Glaring at him, she stiffened. 'You really are the most arrogant man I've ever met.'

'I prefer that to mediocrity,' he said mildly.

Impossible man. Impossible situation. 'I *was* thinking about you—but not in the way you mean.' In for a penny, in for a pound. 'I have to talk to you about something.'

'*Si*? And this something turns your face to one of fear and alarm? This is not good.' He looked at her intently. 'You are a criminal running from the law? Is that it? Or maybe you are here to—how you say?—case the joint? Is that right?' There was amusement in his voice. 'Relax, Cherry. Whatever it is you wish to say, it cannot be so bad.'

She returned his stare mutely, inwardly cursing her weakness in agreeing to Sophia's ridiculous demand.

He had been eating as they talked. Now he pushed his empty dish away from him, saying, 'You are not going to eat your oranges? Not even a bite or two?'

'No. No, thank you.' At the moment they'd choke her.

'Then we will have this so important *conversazione* over coffee on the veranda, *si*?'

Before she could object, he had stood up and moved

round the table to draw her chair away. Taking her arm, he led her through the dining room's French windows and out on to a balcony which ran along the side of the house. It held several comfy chairs and sofas, along with low tables on which citronella candles were burning, presumably to keep away troublesome insects.

Cherry made sure she seated herself in one of the chairs rather than the more intimate sofas. She saw Vittorio's black eyebrows quirk but he said nothing, sitting down opposite her just as Rosa came through the French doors. The maid said something in Italian, to which he answered, '*Si*, Rosa. *Grazie*,' before turning to her and saying, 'The coffee will be here in a few moments.'

Cherry nodded stiffly. She wished it was this time yesterday. A week ago. A month ago. She had accepted this man's hospitality, swum in his pool, eaten his food and drunk his wine, and now she was about to repay his kindness with the sort of news she wouldn't have wanted to spring on her worst enemy. Whatever way you looked at it, it was a bum deal.

Before she could speak, Vittorio said softly, 'Look at the sky, *mia piccola*. It is aflame with stars and glowing with the colours of celestial bodies—a night when starlight throws long shadows on the gardens and the countryside, and makes strange apparitions out of the trees, the buildings and us. A night which reminds us how small and insignificant we are and how timeless is the past and the future.'

Cherry didn't look at the night sky. She looked at Vittorio. And in that moment she knew she was attracted to this handsome, autocratic stranger in a way she had never been attracted to a man before. She had known it from the moment she laid eyes on him, which was why she had fought it so ferociously.

The shadows had carved dark hollows in the male bone structure, but his eyes were glittering granite as he looked into the heavens. And then he turned to her, a self-disparaging smile on his face as he murmured, 'But I digress. What is it you wish to tell me, Cherry from England?'

CHAPTER FIVE

CHERRY was always to remember the next few minutes. They would be burnt into the very fabric of her soul. Rosa stepping through the doors with the coffee. Vittorio pouring her a cup of the rich dark liquid with its fragrant aroma. The scent of the candles and the sudden cry of a startled bird disturbed in its refuge for the night. They all led up to the moment his gaze held hers and he said again, 'Well? What is it?' as he lifted his cup to his lips.

There was a faint ringing in her ears, but she knew she just had to say it, baldly and with no lead-up, or she would lose her nerve. 'It's about Sophia. The reason she has been so difficult for the last month or so—'

'Multiply that by twelve and you are about there,' he interrupted sardonically.

'She is expecting a baby, Vittorio.'

She actually felt the earth shudder on its axis. There followed a moment of complete stillness.

'What did you say?' His voice was flat—curiously flat.

'She and Santo— It wasn't his fault, not really— That is, Sophia said—'

'What did Sophia say, Cherry?'

His face frightened her. 'She is petrified, Vittorio.

She hasn't even told Santo yet, and she insisted it was her fault. She persuaded him. He didn't really want to—'

An explosive few words in Italian followed and Cherry was glad she couldn't speak the language. She stared at him, her eyes huge in her white face, and found it actually pained her to see the agony and an almost boyish vulnerability distorting the hard handsome face.

He stood up, and she said quickly, 'She isn't here. She's gone to see Santo. To tell him about—about the baby.'

He stared down at her, an avenging monochrome in the thick twilight in which stars twinkled above them and all nature seemed hushed and sleepy. It wasn't right to receive such devastating news on a beautiful night like this one, she thought inconsequentially. This was a night for sweet dreams.

After what seemed an eternity, he sat down again. 'Sophia asked you, a stranger, to tell me about her condition?' His voice was icy. 'Why is that?'

'She—she thought that was best.'

'For whom?' The cold voice was scathing.

'Actually for you, as well as her and Santo,' Cherry said honestly. 'She thought you might do something you'd regret in the first moments of knowing and she was seeking to avoid confrontation. I—I think she and Santo are going to come here in a little while to talk to you.'

'Then there will indeed be a confrontation.' His deep voice was low but with a piercing intensity that brought her heart into her throat. 'Rest assured on that.'

She stared at him helplessly, wondering what to say, and then decided she had nothing to lose in stating the truth. 'If you hurt Santo you will lose Sophia for ever. You know that, don't you? Your nephew or niece too. She loves him, Vittorio. She wants nothing more in life than to be his wife and the mother of his child. That's the way it is.'

'Do not speak to me of how it is. What do you know? Before this day you had not even met Sophia,' he bit out furiously, his voice shaking with the force of his emotion.

'I know that, but sometimes a stranger sees things much more clearly simply because they are a stranger and not involved. She knows exactly what she wants and it's not a finishing school.'

'She is a child.'

'No, she isn't.'

It was foolish to argue Sophia's case, she knew that, so why was she doing it? Tomorrow she'd be gone from this house and she would never see Vittorio or Sophia again. The best thing she could do was make her excuses right now and go to bed, let Vittorio do as he saw fit. But if he lost Sophia he would regret it for the rest of his life and it would change him. She didn't know how she had come by the knowledge, but she was sure of it. Deep fires ran in Vittorio and he would love or hate in equal measure.

'Sophia isn't a child,' she repeated earnestly, 'and it's essential you see that right now before it's too late. She wanted to belong to Santo, she orchestrated the event, and although she obviously didn't think she would get pregnant she's nevertheless delighted about it. I'm sorry if that cuts through your picture of your sister, but it's the truth. She was always going to get married one day, Vittorio. It's just happened sooner than expected.'

'She will not marry Santo,' he growled. 'Her life would be one of hard work from dawn to dusk. It is not what my parents would have wished for Sophia.'

'Or perhaps it's not what you would wish for her?' She couldn't believe her temerity, and by the look on

Vittorio's face neither could he. 'But she is a person in her own right, a flesh-and-blood human being, not a possession, and she has chosen her own road. For right or wrong.'

'And if it is wrong?' he ground out bitterly.

'Then all you can do is be there for her.

As she spoke she thought it was almost as though she was talking to a parent about a wayward child, and in a way she supposed it was. Vittorio had brought Sophia up, he had sacrificed his own plans and dreams for her when he had let Caterina go, and he had been both mother and father to his sister for a long time. On top of that he had the burden of trying to fulfil what he imagined his parents would have wanted for their only daughter.

This last thought made her say quietly, 'Your parents would not have wanted their only two children to become estranged, for whatever reason. You must know that, Vittorio.'

'She has brought shame to the Carella name,' he said, dark and angry. 'Giving herself to a man before she is his wife.'

'Oh, for goodness' sake! What matters? Sophia or your stupid name? She isn't the first girl to be in this situation and she won't be the last. If you give her and Santo your blessing they can be married immediately and everyone will think the baby is early—and even if they don't, so what? You don't strike me as the type of man who thinks he has to answer to anyone.'

'How dare you speak to me like this?' His voice was cold steel. 'This is no concern of yours.'

'Sophia made it my concern when she asked me to speak to you.' Cherry forced her tone to remain quiet, although her face burned with heat. How did you get through to a man like Vittorio—a man who thought he was right about everything? 'I didn't want to, I can assure you. I knew exactly how you would react.' Actually, he'd been more calm than she'd expected.

'Is this so?' His glittering eyes locked with hers. 'You think I should be glad that my sixteen-year-old sister has thrown her life away? That she is going to be a mother?'

Swamped by the feeling she was making matters worse and not better, Cherry took a deep breath. 'I know this is not ideal, but it's happened and Sophia wants the baby. She wouldn't agree to an abortion,' she added on a warning note.

'You think I would suggest such a thing?' If he had been angry before he was now livid. 'What kind of man do you think I am? A monster? Is that it?'

If she answered that honestly it would do nothing to defuse the situation. 'I don't know,' she said neutrally. 'As you pointed out earlier, before today I hadn't met you or Sophia. And, believe me, I wish I'd spent the night in the car rather than be in the middle of all this.'

He stared at her, and as he did so she watched him make a huge effort to control his temper. It was clear her words had reminded him she was a guest in his house when he said, 'I must apologise, Cherry. Sophia was wrong to ask of you what she did, but this does not excuse my behaviour.'

His mastery of his emotions was impressive. Taken aback, she murmured awkwardly, 'That's all right. It—it was a shock. And I wanted to help. I still do. If you want me to stay until Sophia and Santo come—'

'That will not be necessary.' It was polite, but rage still simmered under the surface. 'This is not your problem.'

She stood up and he rose too, his manners once again

impeccable. 'Don't push her away,' Cherry said from the heart, without stopping to consider her words—because if she did she wouldn't dare speak them. 'She knows you'll be disappointed and angry, but give her and Santo a chance to talk to you. She loves you very much and this is a time when she needs your help, not rejection. And Santo—he really has been led by her in this.'

'You are asking me to keep my hands off Santo's throat?' he said with a spark of dark humour. 'Is that it?'

'Not just that. The person who said "sticks and stones may break your bones but names will never hurt you" didn't know what they were on about. Words can do deeper harm than any physical blow.' She knew. She had lived with her mother and Angela for many years before she'd been able to make her escape. 'And once said, you can't take them back.'

His eyes narrowed, and he reached out a hand and lifted her chin so she was forced to meet his gaze. 'Why do you care so much about Sophia?' he asked softly. 'You barely know her.'

Her heart was thudding as she felt his strength and warmth flow into her through his fingers, and the delicious smell of him invaded her senses. It was in that moment that she realised it wasn't so much the sister but the brother she was concerned about. Sophia would be fine. She had her Santo and the baby. But Vittorio... And then she told herself not to be so monumentally stupid. If anyone could stand on their own two feet and take what life dished out it was Vittorio Carella.

She shrugged. Vittorio seemed quite unaffected by her closeness, but his nearness was turning her insides to melted butter. 'We're all sisters under the skin,' she managed fairly lightly. 'And I like Sophia. That's all.'

She didn't expect him to bend his head towards her, or the hard sweet kiss that followed. And then he stepped back a pace, steadying her when she swayed slightly. 'Go to bed, Cherry,' he said expressionlessly, his hands leaving her body. 'It has been a long day, *si*? Breakfast is at seven-thirty.'

Vittorio had not prolonged the kiss, so why was it that this man only had to touch her and a wild kind of exhilaration filled her? She didn't even know if she liked him, for goodness' sake. It was humiliating at best and dangerous at worst, but thank goodness he couldn't read her mind.

'Goodnight.' She suddenly needed the safety of her room. 'And—and thank you again for your hospitality.'

He smiled cynically. 'In spite of the fact you would have preferred the peace and quiet of your little car?'

She'd asked for that one, she thought as she turned and left. She glanced back at him before walking into the house. He was standing where she'd left him, gazing over the dark grounds, his big figure dark and brooding.

Go to bed, a little voice at the back of her mind spoke firmly. *You've done all you can. It's up to them now.*

Once in her bedroom she undressed and showered quickly, pulling on one of the two pairs of cotton pyjamas she'd brought with her for the trip before climbing into bed. It was extremely comfortable, but in spite of that she lay staring into the shadowed room, lit only by the moonlight streaming in through the windows. The night sky was black, with myriad tiny stars sparkling like diamonds, and the perfume of the Carella gardens drifted through the window, bathing the room in a soft rich scent. England seemed a million miles away, and Angela and Liam and all the heartache connected with them might have happened in another lifetime. All her thoughts and emotions were tied up with the tall dark man standing, waiting on the veranda, and she found herself praying desperately he wouldn't do or say anything he would regret.

What happened in this family shouldn't really matter. They were nothing to her after all. She had only known Vittorio and his sister for a matter of hours, and she hadn't even met Santo, but in spite of telling herself this over and over again she couldn't deny the fact it did matter. Terribly. Which was crazy. She wrinkled her nose at herself. Crazy woman, that was her.

She lay, her ears straining for any sound which would indicate Sophia and Santo were downstairs, but the night was quiet. Maybe Sophia had gone to see Santo and he wasn't at home? Or perhaps she had told him about the baby and he wanted nothing to do with her? Or it could be that the pair of them had come to the house and Vittorio had thrown Santo off the property? But she would have heard the sound of raised voices, surely? Or maybe Sophia was too frightened to return?

These and a hundred and one other possibilities went round and round in her head until it began to ache. Giving up all hope of sleep, she slid out of bed and walked over to the windows, stepping out on to the balcony which was still warm from the heat of the day. Sitting down, she sighed softly. It was beautiful and so peaceful here, she thought idly. Not like the *pensioni* in Lecce, where the suitor of the young Italian girl in the house next door had used to rev up his Vespa under her window each night before leaving, presumably to impress her. This followed the same philosophy of every young Italian male to prove his voice, motor-bicycle or radio to be louder than anyone else's—the necessity of cutting a dash was of prime importance, she reflected ruefully.

Cherry shifted in the chair, leaning her elbows on the stone surround of the balcony as she drank in the perfumed air.

But then, she thought on, it was hardly surprising that the Italians were a people of strong emotions, living as they did in a land of such powerfully distinct colours. Azure sky, cobalt sea, golden sunshine, silver olives, green vines, red brick, white marble—the list was endless. She had read somewhere before starting on her journey that the three major active volcanoes on the entire continent were all situated in Italy, and since arriving on its shores that didn't surprise her. In fact it was fitting for such a fiery, passionate race. She just hoped the simmering volcano in the shape of Vittorio downstairs didn't explode tonight.

She sat on for another hour or more, until she found herself dozing in the chair and returned to bed. She was on the verge of falling asleep when she heard a soft knock at her door. Sure it was Sophia, she flung back the light covers and padded barefoot across the room, opening the door quietly.

'Did I wake you?' Vittorio was leaning against the far wall, hands thrust in his pockets and his expression hidden in the shadows. 'Were you asleep?'

So surprised her voice came out in a squeak, she managed to say, 'No, I wasn't quite asleep,' and she wished with all her heart she was wearing an alluring feminine nightie rather than her sensible cotton pyjamas dotted with fat little teddy bears. She must look like a schoolgirl.

'In view of your concern for Sophia I thought you might still be awake.' His voice was soft, but he didn't move from his position some feet away. 'I wanted to re-assure you that Santo has left the house intact. Just,' he added darkly.

'They came to see you? I didn't hear them,' she said guilelessly, before blushing as she realised she'd given away her desire to eavesdrop. Great spy she'd make.

If he'd noticed, he didn't comment. 'There is to be a meeting of the two families tomorrow, but that is not what I came to tell you.' He levered himself off the wall and came closer, and it was all she could do not to step back a pace. 'Sophia wishes you to stay for a while.' His eyes were black in the shadows, his handsome face without expression. 'There is a great deal to arrange very quickly if she is going to marry Santo before her condition becomes obvious, and the enormity of it has overwhelmed her. She has no mother or sister, no female confidante, and at such a time...' He shrugged. 'She does not have the rapport with my housekeeper, and in the matter of shopping for a wedding dress, a trousseau...'

Shock rendered her speechless for a moment. Swallowing hard, she looked at him wide-eyed. 'But she must have friends? And didn't you say there is a grandmother?'

'Our grandmother is ninety years old,' he said drily, 'and, whilst she would not thank me for saying so, arrangements of this kind would be beyond her. As for friends—' again the shrug '—Sophia wants you. I understand she is to put the request to you tomorrow morning, but I felt it only fair that you have some time to consider such an undertaking. I am very aware this is your holiday, but your remark about being sisters under the skin...'

Again his voice died away, but this time Cherry peered at him more closely. If she wasn't mistaken, her soft heart was being played on here. 'But...' She paused, hopelessly out of her depth. 'Sophia doesn't *know* me.' The suggestion was ridiculous, absolutely ridiculous, so why was she considering it for even a second?

He shifted position slightly and every nerve in her body responded. 'Do you not think that sometimes you can know more about someone in five minutes than five years with someone else?' he murmured very, very gently.

He was so close now the warm fragrance of the aftershave she'd smelt earlier was teasing her senses. 'I'm— I'm not even Italian,' she protested, as though that was news to him.

He brushed aside the feeble prevarication. 'That is of no importance. Sophia knows what will be required. You would merely provide a helping hand, listen to any problems and support her—even lend a shoulder to cry on if necessary. I understand women can get very emotional at such an important time, and in view of her condition it is best she is kept as calm as possible, *si*? But of course the decision is yours.'

She stared at him. This man was sex on legs, and if she wasn't careful she could find herself in a whole heap of trouble here—a case of out of Liam's frying pan and into Vittorio's fire. Because one thing was certain. Vittorio Carella could have any woman he wanted with a click of his aristocratic fingers, and if—*if*—he was of a mind to dally a little with her, it wouldn't mean a thing to him.

Of course she could be completely on the wrong track. Nevertheless... 'I don't think—'

'Do not make your decision now, Cherry.' He straightened, and her stomach muscles clenched. 'Sleep on it. Isn't that what you English say?'

'Vittorio—'

'And do not be influenced by the fact that Sophia is

all alone at such a time,' he continued, with what Cherry considered shameless manipulation. 'She will manage. Somehow.'

From breathing fire and damnation he had done a one-hundred-and-eighty-degree turn, hadn't he? Forcing herself to ignore the tantalising glimpse of dark body hair where the first couple of buttons of his shirt were undone, she said, 'Do I take it you are prepared to give Sophia and Santo your blessing?'

The firm mouth hardened for a moment. 'Blessing is stretching my benevolence somewhat. But…' He hesitated. 'I do not want to lose her. Or, as you pointed out, my nephew or niece. Santo…' again he hesitated '…is not strong enough for her. Sophia is a Carella. She is obstinate and headstrong and sure she is always right. These qualities have taken the males in my family to a position of wealth and power, but Sophia is a woman. She must see Santo as the head of the family or the marriage will not be happy.'

Cherry reared up as though she'd been bitten. 'Excuse *me*?' she said hotly. 'You aren't seriously saying that Sophia has to treat Santo as her lord and master once they're married, are you?'

Vittorio surveyed her coolly. 'I am saying that I would have preferred Sophia to make a match that is more equal. A man has to know how to handle someone like Sophia, and I am not sure yet that Santo can.'

'They love each other. Surely that is all that matters in the long run? They'll sort out their relationship in their own way.' She glared at him. 'It might not be exactly how you think it should be, but you could actually be wrong, you know.'

'My, my, my.' His voice was soft, silky, but with an

edge to it. 'Is this one of the things you are passionate about, *mia piccola*? Along with animals, reading, and eating out with friends, of course.'

Sarcastic swine. Refusing to be drawn, she took a deep breath and told herself to calm down. 'I believe men and women are equal, if that's what you are asking.'

'This is good. I, too, think this.'

'You?' How could he have the nerve to say that?

'But of course. The sexes are different—different needs, different strengths and weaknesses—but in a perfect union the two fit together as one and complement the whole. Each has their role to play.'

Cherry stared at him suspiciously. 'You said Sophia should regard Santo as the head; that's not equality.'

'I disagree.' He propped one arm against the doorpost, his fingers splayed next to her head.

His rich masculine fragrance invaded her space and caused her nerves to jolt, even as she told herself to keep perfectly still and composed.

'Santo will love and honour Sophia and put her before anyone, even their children, and Sophia will respect and support him in his role of husband and father and understand that the responsibility for taking care of her and their family can be a heavy one. That is how it should be.' His voice dropped an octave and he bent a little closer. 'You think differently?'

She was having a job to think at all. His close proximity was intoxicating. He wasn't touching her with any part of himself and yet she was melting. Somehow she managed to keep her voice from shaking when she said, skirting his question, 'Some couples both work at responsible jobs and bring an equal amount of money into the household. There's no "head" as such.'

'Wrong. A true man will always see his woman as the weaker vessel and do everything he can to love and protect her, allow her to be the person she is meant to be even at the cost of his own wellbeing. Women are softer, gentler, more…easily broken.'

She shivered inside. 'That's male stereotyping.'

'No, *mia piccola*,' he murmured softly. 'It is a truth as ancient as time, and when either sex fights against it, it is a prelude to disaster. There is a time for both man and woman to give and take. Like now, for instance…'

She had known he was going to kiss her, had wanted him to, and now she trembled as he took her lips in a long, slow, leisurely exploration that sent a flood of sensation running through her veins. The kiss deepened, his probing tongue invading the sweetness of her mouth with masterful ease as he moved her into him, his fingertips against her lower ribs, his palms cupping her sides.

She felt her fingers lock behind the muscled neck and as they stroked the crisp short hair Vittorio sighed raggedly against her lips before his mouth plundered hers again, this time more fiercely.

He was so, so good at this—so experienced, so sure. The thought was there but it wasn't enough to make her pull away, even though she knew she must be just one woman in many he had made love to. He growled low in his throat, the sound finding an echo within herself as her heart hammered against her ribs and a slow throb in the core of her intensified.

His hands moved upwards, sliding beneath her pyjama top, and as she felt his fingers on her skin it acted as an injection of reality, breaking the sensuous web. She jerked away, suddenly aware of what she was allowing. *This man was a stranger. She hadn't even known him twenty-four hours and she was virtually offering herself on a plate. She was no better than Angela. Worse.* It was the wake-up call she needed.

Taking another step backwards into the bedroom, she said shakily, 'I—I can't do this. I'm—I'm sorry.'

'Because of the man you left England to escape?' he said softly. 'He still has your heart?'

Oh, he was good. She'd give him that. He didn't miss a trick. 'I told you. I'm not escaping anyone.' She drew air into her lungs. 'And even if I was it wouldn't alter the fact that I don't sleep around.'

'I did not think for a minute that you would, Cherry.'

The way he said her name in his delicious accent caused another shiver inside, but her voice was tight when she said, 'I didn't come to Italy looking for a cheap holiday romance, if that's what you're thinking.'

He tilted his head. 'Why would I think that, *mia piccola*?' He was standing in the doorway now, leaning nonchalantly against the frame, and the very casualness of his pose brought a flood of pride to her rescue.

He could clearly take her or leave her, she told herself bitterly. Like all men, it would seem. And that was fine—just fine. She could do exactly the same. 'I just wanted to make my position absolutely clear.' She tried to moderate her stare into less of a glare. 'Should I agree to your sister's request.'

He nodded. 'Understood.' And with that he stepped back on to the landing and closed the door, leaving her alone with an abruptness that was shocking.

CHAPTER SIX

SHE'D deserved the sleepless night, Cherry told herself the next morning, after she had watched the night hours creep by. She'd been unbelievably stupid to allow Vittorio to kiss her like that and kiss him back. Of course he had expected he could go further. He'd probably thought they'd both spend the night in her bed—well, his bed, to be pedantic about it. She was in his house after all.

But not for much longer. She nodded to the thought as she stepped out of the shower and began to dry her hair. It was seven o'clock on a beautiful May morning and with any luck the hire car would be delivered before long. Of course there was breakfast to endure before that, but she'd get through and leave as soon as she could.

She'd go and see the Castel del Monte first; several people had mentioned it was the finest castle in the region and a breathtaking monument to the modern eye. And then she'd travel further up the coast to the province of Foggia and see more castles, churches and cathedrals. Someone had told her—she couldn't remember who— that just outside Foggia were the remains of the largest Roman amphitheatre in southern Italy, with a vast arena which had accommodated twenty thousand spectators; she couldn't leave the area without paying a visit. A few days of culture and improving her mind was just what she needed to put the last twenty-four hours firmly behind her.

She continued her plans as she dressed, refusing to think of anything else, and left her room just before seven-thirty to make her way to the breakfast room. The door was open when she reached it, and on entering she saw the big dark figure of Vittorio sitting at the table reading a paper. Sophia was not present, which wasn't what she'd hoped.

'*Buongiorno*, Cherry.' Vittorio had risen and pulled out a chair for her before she was halfway across the room, and she had no choice but to sit down next to him.

She sat, refusing to acknowledge that he looked just as good in jeans and a T-shirt as the more tailored clothes he'd been wearing the day before—although the jeans and T-shirt shouted *exclusivity* anyway. Born with the proverbial silver spoon and spoiled rotten from the cradle, she told herself viciously. He had no idea of what real life was like. None at all. She doubted he had ever done a day's work in his life.

'I trust you slept well?' he said softly, interrupting her character assassination.

Wild horses wouldn't have dragged the truth from her. 'Very well, thank you,' she replied stiffly, as the two maids bustled in with large dishes of food, which they placed on a long sideboard at the side of the room.

'It is customary that we help ourselves in the morning,' Vittorio explained quietly. 'Rosa and Gilda will bring coffee. Would you prefer espresso or cappuccino?'

Cherry turned to Rosa, who was waiting at her side. 'Cappuccino, please.'

'*Si, signorina.*'

The maid's smile was sunny. She clearly couldn't detect the tension in the air, although to Cherry the atmosphere was positively crackling. She helped herself to a glass of orange juice from the jug on the table and sipped it as the two girls left the room. Every morning since arriving in Italy she had woken up looking forward to breakfast. Today her stomach felt in knots.

'There was a call from the car hire firm this morning, Cherry.' Vittorio rose to his feet as he spoke, coming behind her and pulling back her chair for her as she stood up, before handing her a plate. 'They regret that due to circumstances outside of their control they cannot provide a replacement car until tomorrow.'

'What?' Her surprise caused her to meet the beautiful grey eyes for the first time that morning and she felt the impact right down to her toes.

'I told them it is not a problem,' he continued smoothly. 'And they can deliver the car the same time tomorrow morning, OK?'

Not OK. *So* not OK. Vittorio was waiting for her to select food from the dishes on display but, ignoring them, she said, 'I want a car today. I'm not prepared to wait. It's in the agreement I signed that a new car will be provided within twenty-four hours. Did you remind them of that?'

'You are bristling like the porcupine,' he said mildly. 'I take it you are not willing to help Sophia and stay for a while?'

She turned away, swallowing hard and pretending to examine the dishes of sweet pastries and preserves, along with others of salami and cheeses, fresh fruit cut into slices and arranged in a colourful pattern, and bowls of olives. 'I don't think I'd be much help.' If anything had convinced her she needed to leave this house as quickly as possible it was Vittorio, freshly shaved, damp hair slicked back and smelling like heaven. This was self-preservation, clear and simple. *Ignore it at your peril, Cherry.*

'I do not think this is so, but of course the choice is yours and yours alone.' Vittorio was filling his plate, apparently indifferent to her decision. 'Ah, here is Sophia,' he added, looking beyond Cherry.

Cherry turned quickly. She had half expected Vittorio's sister to be bright and bouncy now the truth was out in the open and Vittorio had taken it as well as could be expected, but Sophia's lovely face was tear-stained and her expression woebegone.

Instinctively Cherry put down her plate and went to the young girl, taking Sophia's arm as she said quietly, 'What's wrong?'

'Has Vittorio told you the wedding is to take place in a few weeks?' Sophia's green eyes were swimming with tears. 'I do not know where to start, Cherry. And I was sick this morning.' A tear slipped down one cheek. 'I do not feel well.'

'You should have thought of that before you seduced Santo,' said Vittorio behind them, with what Cherry considered utter callousness. 'You have no one but yourself to blame for the position you are in. You said that yourself yesterday.'

'You're not helping.' Cherry swung round and glared at him. 'Can't you see she's upset? And it takes two to tango, as you well know.'

'If Sophia had merely indulged in the tango with Santo we would not be having this conversation.' Grey eyes dared her to argue further.

Never one to refuse a challenge, Cherry snorted her

disgust. 'For goodness' sake, we're not all robots like you. Some of us have feelings and Sophia is very tender right now. Your sister's having a baby, and that's a huge change in a woman's body and emotions. She needs your understanding—if you have any, that is. Which is very doubtful.'

'My understanding tells me Sophia needs to sit down,' Vittorio said drily.

Cherry's gaze shot back to his sister, who was looking green. By the time she had ushered Sophia back to bed, telling her to sleep as late as she could and then have something to eat when she was rested, Cherry knew she was hooked. Sophia had asked her to stay for a little while and help her with the preparations for the wedding, as Vittorio had predicted, and there was just something incredibly vulnerable about this child-woman who had lost her parents at such a tragically young age. And Sophia had been so sympathetic and kind down by the pool, when she had confided about Liam and Angela. If she stayed to help Sophia now it would be just a month or so out of her life. She could give the Italian girl that, and would do so gladly if it wasn't for Vittorio. But she could handle him. Or, more precisely, this ridiculous attraction she felt. And maybe she wouldn't see much of him anyway—not if she was helping Sophia with the organisation of the wedding.

Vittorio's gaze was waiting for her when she walked back into the breakfast room. She saw her plate was in its place on the table and a steaming mug of cappuccino by the side of it.

'Have you always been such a little mother?' he asked softly.

It could have been sarcastic but it wasn't. She relaxed

infinitesimally as she sat down. 'Always,' she said, a little ruefully. Any lame ducks, be they human or animal, always seemed to make a beeline for her door. She had even started dating Liam after he'd cried on her shoulder after his former girlfriend had unceremoniously dumped him.

Vittorio nodded. 'The porcupine with the soft centre. I like this. Too often I have found it is the other way round with modern women.'

She eyed him over her cappuccino as she took a sip, but said nothing. She was feeling a little shattered, to be truthful.

'You think I am hard, unkind, *si*?' he murmured. 'Unfair?'

If she was going to be around for a while she might as well be honest. 'Certainly cynical,' she said, without denying the other words.

He didn't seem offended. Surveying her thoughtfully, he leaned back in his chair and sipped his coffee. 'I think you are right,' he said after a moment or two. 'But I do not consider cynicism a bad thing on the whole—not if it is hand-in-hand with fairness and impartiality. The only danger can be if it sours an individual so that he or she cannot recognise true genuineness when it is presented to them.'

Cherry stared at him. 'And can you?' she asked bluntly. 'Recognise the real thing, I mean?'

Something flared in the grey eyes before his lids came down to conceal his gaze for a second. When he looked at her again it was gone. 'But of course.'

'Of course,' she agreed derisively. 'Silly of me to ask. It must be wonderful to be so amazingly clever.'

'It has been that way for so long that I do not even

think about it,' he said gravely. 'But, *si*, you are right again. It is wonderful.'

She tried not to smile, she really did—his ego was big enough already—but she couldn't help herself.

'That is better,' he said contentedly. 'You were in danger of giving yourself indigestion with all that acidity. Now, eat your breakfast, Cherry, and then we must make the call to your car people, *si*?' He smiled innocently. 'To insist on a vehicle?'

He knew. She wasn't sure *how* he knew she'd changed her mind about leaving, but she was positive he did. She ate a pastry before she said, 'Actually, I shan't need a car today after all. I've told Sophia I'll at least think about staying for a bit and talk to her later. I'll phone and postpone delivery.'

'Really?' The grey eyes opened wider in simulated surprise.

Yes, really, Mr Know-All. 'But I've made no promises.'

'Of course not.' It was soothing. And irritating.

'And if I do stay it can only be for a short time, until Sophia is feeling more in control.'

'Absolutely.' He nodded thoughtfully.

'She is very emotional at the moment.'

'As is to be expected,' he agreed gravely.

Cherry admitted defeat and ate her breakfast, aware Vittorio was watching her with silent amusement. But it wasn't that which was causing the flutterings in her stomach. More the fact that now she'd made up her mind to stay she knew she would have found it a huge wrench to leave this morning. Which confirmed all her fears. Stupid, stupid, stupid.

She had almost finished eating when Vittorio spoke again. 'I think Sophia will sleep for some time. She is certainly over-tired and will wish to be composed for the meeting with Santo's family this evening. I am visiting our factory this morning. Would you like to accompany me and see for yourself how the Carella olive oil is produced? It will while away an hour or two,' he added offhandedly.

Cherry hesitated. She was genuinely interested in seeing first-hand the process which made Puglia the main olive oil centre in Italy, but it seemed a little too…cosy somehow. Then she told herself she was being ridiculous. If she stayed on for a while she had to be able to be around Vittorio; perhaps there was no time like the present to get used to it and master her body's response to his particular brand of vigorous masculinity? 'Thank you,' she said politely. 'I'd like that.'

'I will meet you outside in fifteen minutes.'

Vittorio was sitting in a gleaming black Range Rover when she walked down the steps of the villa, the morning sun already blazing hot in the cloudless blue sky. She was wearing a sleeveless pink cotton dress that she'd had for ages, but it was lovely and cool on a warm day, and she had pulled her hair into a high knot so the air could get to the back of her neck. Already she felt sticky. Vittorio looked cool and comfortable and much, *much* too good-looking.

He slid out of the car as she approached, opening the passenger door and helping her inside the vehicle with the natural courtesy she'd noticed before. She felt flustered and hot as she sat down, but now the heat came from within rather than without. She exhaled slowly as Vittorio walked round the large bonnet and then stared primly ahead as he joined her in the Range Rover. She caught a faint whiff of his aftershave, the elusive and

evocative scent which she now associated with him, and
her nerves responded, tightening and vibrating.

'So.' He started the engine, swinging the vehicle in
a semi-circle before leaving the pebbled area in front of
the villa and joining the road they'd travelled on the day
before, but in the opposite direction from where her little car sat marooned. 'What do you know of the liquid
gold we harvest?'

Trying to match his casualness, Cherry smiled. 'It's
great for dressing salads and grilling meat?'

'Si.' He grinned, and her traitorous body responded.
'But there is much more to the oil than that—as I am sure
you have heard. It is beneficial in fighting heart disease
and obesity, and this was understood even in ancient
times. Roman and Greek athletes were known to smear
the olive oil over their bodies to improve bloodflow and
enhance muscle development, and in some parts of the
world this still happens today.'

Cherry had a mental image of that magnificent body
she had practically drooled over at the pool the day before gleaming and oiled and had to swallow hard.

'And of course today the oil is used not just in cooking
but in a wide range of cosmetics and soap, and for this
the Puglia region is superb. All our oil is extra-virgin—
the best quality, *si*? Less than one per cent of acidity per
hundred grams. And a beautiful yellow. The colour of
the sun.' He grinned again. 'But I am the bore. This cannot interest you, Cherry.'

Whatever else Vittorio was, he could never be boring. She glanced at the large strong hands on the steering
wheel, the gold watch on his tanned wrist glittering in
the sunshine, and tried to keep her voice steady. 'On the
contrary. I find it very interesting to think an industry

that started thousands of years ago is still going strong and is growing more successful if anything. And even I can tell Puglia's oil is better than what I've been used to at home. Before I came to Italy I would never have dreamt of enjoying a basket of local bread dipped in olive oil as lunch, but it's delicious.'

'*Si*—and healthy. We make good *bambini*—strong sons and daughters, us Italians—and we enjoy life.'

She dared not let her thoughts go down that route, and as the white-walled, red-roofed buildings of the Carella factory came into view, breathed a silent sigh of relief.

Vittorio's manager met them as he brought the Range Rover to a standstill. His name was Federico and he was a cousin of Vittorio's. It appeared all the dozen or so employees were family. While Vittorio disappeared into the office, Federico escorted her round the factory, where modern machinery had replaced the traditional presses of Vittorio's grandfather's day, taking Cherry through the labour-intensive and, in its early stages, back-breaking work needed to process the oil. First the trees must be harvested, he explained, and then—swiftly so that the olives didn't bruise, oxidise or spoil in any way—the fruit must be pulped to a paste. The paste then had to be stirred vigorously before the final method of extraction was performed.

'And all must be done with love, *si*?' Federico said with a flash of his dark brown eyes. 'This makes the best olive oil.'

Cherry smiled, amused by the mild flirting as she wondered if anything at all was done in Italy without the *loooove* factor! It would appear not.

Vittorio was waiting for them at the foot of the stairs which led up to the office after the tour, his hands thrust into the pockets of his jeans and his grey eyes fastened on her face.

Federico grinned at his cousin as they reached him. 'This woman is not merely the pretty face,' he said appreciatively. 'Cherry has asked the questions of intelligence, *si*?'

'I'm glad you approve,' Vittorio drawled drily. 'I've signed those documents you left on my desk, and the papers for the next shipments are with them. There is nothing else of importance?' And as Federico shook his head, 'Then I will see you tomorrow.'

'You are not taking Cherry away so soon?' Federico protested.

'Cherry.' Vittorio turned to her, his eyes dancing. 'This man has a wife and a houseful of little ones. Do not be fooled by his velvet tongue. He is the Casanova.'

They left Federico still objecting, and once in the Range Rover Vittorio slid one arm along the back of her seat as he turned to her. 'There is no rush to get back.' His eyes lingered on her hair and he murmured, almost to himself, 'Such colours when the light catches it. Red, gold—like the flames of a fire. It shimmers like silk in the sun, do you know this? It is a crime to imprison such loveliness.'

She felt his fingers release the clip holding her hair, and as it fell about her shoulders Cherry jerked away. 'Don't,' she said sharply, holding out her hand for the fastener. 'It's too hot to wear it down today.'

'And is this the only reason you hide such beauty from me?' he said, ignoring her outstretched fingers.

She stared at him, wondering if he was making fun of her. Her hair was ordinary. *She* was ordinary. OK, so she wouldn't exactly shatter mirrors, and when she took the time to dress up and do her hair and make-up with more care than usual she could pass for averagely attractive, but that was all. She had no illusions about herself, and if she had had, Angela and her mother would have set her right years ago.

'My hair is nothing special.' She fixed him with her most severe look. 'And how I choose to wear it has absolutely nothing to do with you.'

He smiled faintly, which Cherry found incredibly irritating. 'Have you always been so defensive or is it a barrier erected since the disappointment in love?' he asked with unforgivable audacity. 'And do not deny once again there is not a man behind your sojourn in my country. Sophia has told me otherwise.'

Whether the quick stab of hurt at Sophia's betrayal was evident in her face Cherry didn't know, but in the next breath Vittorio said, 'That is all she said. No details. Not one. And she only told me that because she was anxious I did not... What is that English phrase? Ah, *si*. Put my foot in it in some way.'

She had recovered enough to glare at him. 'Your sister clearly doesn't know you as well as she thinks she does,' she bit out, 'if she imagines a little thing like knowing someone has been hurt would stop you barging in where angels fear to tread.'

'But I am no angel, *mia piccola*.' To add insult to injury, he tucked the hairclip away in the pocket on his side of the vehicle as he added, 'And a man who is stupid enough to let you slip through his fingers does not deserve you anyway. Now, I am going to take you to lunch in Locorotondo, and afterwards we will visit the Baroque cathedral. Sophia will sleep for most of the day, I am sure. Now the secret she had been worrying about for weeks is out in the open she is feeling something of a reaction, I think. But tomorrow she will have to begin to consider all the preparations for the wedding, and you will be needed.'

Fighting the urge to scream at him, Cherry drew on all her considerable will-power to stay cool and composed. 'I have no intention of having lunch with you. I agreed to stay to help Sophia.'

'Which I have no doubt you will do admirably.' He started the engine. 'But today I show you the *città del vino bianco*, Locorotondo—the city of white wine— while you are still the tourist sightseeing rather than Sophia's aide. This will be a pleasant and relaxing inter- lude before your hard word, *si*?'

No. Definitely not relaxing, and with her jangled nerves, probably not pleasant either. She would far rather go back to the house and spend the time by the pool with just a book for company. She opened her mouth to argue further, glanced at Vittorio's imperturbable profile, and shut it again. He'd made up his mind, and although she might not have known him very long she knew once made up it wouldn't change. Short of throwing herself out of the Range Rover she had no choice but to accom- pany him.

That wouldn't be so bad if a secret part of her didn't want it so badly. Which was dangerous. Very danger- ous. And foolish. Vittorio must have had lots of women, and would continue to have them; he was experienced, worldly-wise and devastatingly charismatic—and if love ever featured in his life in the future the woman con- cerned would have to be super-special, like him, for it to work.

And then she caught her thoughts in alarm. What

on earth was she thinking about love for? Her cheeks burned. Thank goodness he couldn't read her mind. She had to pull herself together. The sexual attraction she felt for this man was controllable, it had to be, and that was all it was. Once the next few weeks were over and Sophia was settled, life would go on for Vittorio and his sister and they probably wouldn't think of her when she was out of their lives. Vittorio was a man. He could sleep with a woman and move on without emotional difficulty. That was just the way it was. She had to remember that. *She had to remember that.*

CHAPTER SEVEN

CHERRY found one of the charms of Locorotondo was the approach to the town as they drove through the Valle d'Itria, a striking Italian landscape of luxuriant vineyards sleeping in the hot sun and traditional *trulli* houses, where the sweet aroma of the mint growing by the roadside filled the car with its perfume.

Vittorio told her that the dry white *spumante* wine which was a speciality of the area had given the town its nickname and was of the highest quality, but as they got nearer, and she could see the domes of the cathedral, she realised it was an outstandingly beautiful town too. Blindingly white limestone houses and narrow alleyways bedecked with geraniums and citrus plants wound in true Italian style around squares and tiny palm-sheltered courtyards, and by the time Vittorio had parked the Range Rover and they'd wandered on foot deeper into the town and made their way to the cathedral Cherry was smitten.

The cathedral was as magnificent as she had expected, but when they left its confines and Vittorio casually took her hand as she stumbled over some ancient cobbles all she could think about was his fingers holding hers. And he didn't seem inclined to let go. She felt dwarfed by his solid maleness as they walked, but it was an intoxicating feeling, and just for a while—she told herself—she'd enjoy the sensation. It didn't mean anything, she was fully aware of that, so no harm done.

They found a small *trattoria*—an informal restaurant serving simple meat and pasta dishes—and ate sitting outside under a large umbrella, sipping glasses of *spumante* wine. Cherry kept darting quick glances at Vittorio from under her eyelashes, unable to believe she was sitting in the sunshine enjoying a meal with one of the most gorgeous men she had ever seen in her life when just a couple of days before she had been very much on her own. This was the sort of thing that happened to other people, not to her. And it wasn't as if Puglia was a beach resort type of place, where romances were more likely to occur.

Not that this *was* a romance, she reminded herself firmly. Not remotely. She'd made up her mind before leaving England that it would be a very long time before she made the mistake of trusting a man again. It had been one of the reasons she'd decided to spend some months exploring archaeological sites and museums on the continent—places that recalled days of Greek and Roman inhabitants, medieval castles and fortresses, the breathtaking artistry of eighteenth-century Baroque architecture and the rest of the wealth of history countries like Italy, Greece and Turkey contained. She'd wanted to immerse herself in the past and forget the disappointments of the present and the uncertainty of the future, and definitely—*definitely*—steer clear of the male of the species.

She suddenly became aware that Vittorio was sitting gazing at her, having finished his meal, his grey eyes thoughtful. 'You are thinking of this man again.' It was a statement, not a question. 'There is sadness in your face.'

Taken aback, she spoke without thinking. 'I wasn't thinking of Liam. Not specifically.'

'Liam.' A hardness came into his voice. 'I do not like this name.'

It was such a ridiculous thing to say she found herself smiling. 'In spite of what you think, I *am* actually over him,' she said firmly. 'It was a salutary lesson in being foolish enough to place one's trust in a man if nothing else.'

Vittorio finished the last of the wine in his glass before speaking. 'And this is the woman who took me to task for my observations of the female sex yesterday?' he said silkily. 'Such hypocrisy.'

'Not at all.' Hell, she'd walked into that one. 'You were saying women are driven by a man's wealth first and foremost and marry for money, and that's just not true.'

'Forgive me if I misunderstood,' he went on, in the same tone as before, 'but did you not just condemn men as being intrinsically undependable and untrustworthy? Speaking purely for myself, I think it is fair to say you have a limited knowledge of me, and I fail to see how you can make an accurate observation of my character—not to mention all the millions of men out there you have not met.' Black eyebrows rose mockingly. 'Is this not true?'

'Oh…' She was furious with him for catching her out so expertly, and knew she didn't have a leg to stand on in this particular altercation. 'You don't understand what I meant.'

'No?' His smile died. 'But I do know this man let you down in some way, and I would like to know what happened,' he said with utter seriousness.

Something in his voice—a tenderness, maybe?—
caught her unawares and changed the nature of the conversation.

'If you can bring yourself to talk about it, that is.'

'I told you. I'm over him,' she repeated quietly.

'But there is still sadness and even disillusionment.
Your own words prove this.'

Cherry shrugged. The last thing she wanted to do
was reveal how easily Angela had enticed Liam into her
clutches. There was an ignominiousness to it all that still
smarted. But perhaps it would be easier to tell Vittorio
if she was going to be around for a few weeks? If nothing else, it would convince him she had no intention of
going from the frying pan into the fire and that any kind
of dalliance with him was out of the question.

She kept her eyes on the dazzling white wall of the
house opposite them across the cobbled road, the blazing sunlight turning its window boxes of brilliant red
geraniums so bright the contrast was unreal, and began
to speak. She told him it all. It seemed pointless not to.
And it didn't take very long. When she'd finished she
still didn't look at Vittorio straight away, reaching for her
glass and taking a long sip of her wine before she raised
her eyes to his. They were waiting for her.

'I have known women like your sister,' he said softly.
'Just one or two. Predatory females who are never satisfied with what they have. I have the feeling Liam has
got exactly what he deserves. She will make his life hell.
You know this?'

Cherry nodded. Yes, she knew it. She had seen it happen before. But the strange thing was the men concerned
still wanted Angela no matter what she did. It was as
though she injected a love drug into their system and they

were addicted from the first kiss. To her knowledge, not one of Angela's conquests had ever thrown her over. It was always the other way round.

'These people are shallow and without foundation,' Vittorio went on. 'Unable to feel deep emotion and incapable of contentment. Every generation breeds a few of both sexes and it is your misfortune to have one as your sister. They make everyone they come into contact with miserable eventually. It can be no other way. But her power will be defused when you show her you know what she is and that she cannot hurt you or influence you.'

'But she can hurt me,' Cherry pointed out. 'She has. Often.'

'Only because you let her,' he said, very gently. 'And Liam was not the man for you or he would have been immune to her wiles. Love can cut through the power these people exert like a knife through warm butter.'

It was all very well for him to say that. He didn't know Angela or her mother, and he hadn't grown up in Angela's shadow like she had. The very concept was inconceivable to him.

'Your mother? She is not a happy woman?' Vittorio asked perceptively.

Cherry thought about it and realised with a little jolt of surprise that her mother was far from happy. 'No,' she admitted.

'Because all the time she is trying to reconcile what she wants her daughter to be and what she knows deep in her heart she is. No doubt your sister plays your mother's heart like a violin. As I said, these people cause everyone who is close to them to suffer in one way or another.'

Cherry drank the last of her wine just as the waiter appeared with the two espressos Vittorio had ordered.

Once they were alone again, Vittorio looked at her with a small smile playing round his lips. 'Wondering how I know so much about such people, *mia piccola*?'

His question so accurately reflected what she was thinking that she suppressed a nod of agreement.

'It is because I had a lucky escape from one such woman a long time ago,' he said softly, without waiting for her to speak. 'For a short while I thought my heart was broken. It was not, of course. And then events transpired which caused me to reflect that a tongue that carries the sweetness of nectar can be a fatal trap to the unsuspecting bee, rather than a source of life and joy—especially when that tongue is in a beautiful face with an enchanting body to accompany it.'

Was he talking about this Caterina Sophia had mentioned? The woman he'd been about to marry when his parents were killed and who'd then married one of his friends? It was on the tip of her tongue to ask but she couldn't quite bring herself to do so. Instead she sipped her espresso before she said lightly—in a deliberate attempt to break what had become a disturbingly intimate atmosphere—'So now you go from flower to flower and never linger too long?'

He didn't join in her casualness. 'Not exactly.'

He didn't elaborate, and she felt like a child who'd spoken out of turn. She wondered how it was that this man always seemed to put her in the wrong even when she was right.

The stubbornly immovable custom of the siesta was drawing near, and in the next moment or two the waiter appeared with their bill. They left the little *trattoria* and made their way back to the Range Rover, and this time Vittorio did not take her hand. Cherry wondered why she felt bereft and told herself not to be so stupid, at the same time berating herself for agreeing to stay at the Carella villa. She'd made some bad decisions in her life but this had to be the worst.

Once in the vehicle, Vittorio turned to her. 'I have not met your sister, *mia piccola*, but of one thing I am sure. She does not have the beauty of her sibling. You are beautiful, whatever you think to the contrary.' He leaned forward, tipping her chin up with his forefinger and kissing her lightly, trailing his lips across hers before settling himself into his seat and starting the engine.

Cherry couldn't have moved if she had wanted to. She closed her eyes for a moment as they got underway, willing herself to keep still and pretend nothing had happened. She didn't want to be attracted to this dark, volatile stranger who curiously didn't feel a stranger; she couldn't let herself go down that route. He lived in one world and she in another; they were different in every way. He had a magnetism that would draw women from puberty to old age. She—well, she was Cherry Gibbs from England, unremarkable, conventional, no great shakes. That was reality. That was fact. Even if they began something—her stomach did a cartwheel—she would be a ship that passed in the night as far as he was concerned. Whereas for her…

'You are very quiet.' He glanced swiftly at her before returning his gaze to the road ahead.

Cherry mustered all her will-power to lie convincingly. 'I was thinking about Sophia. I hope she's feeling better.'

'Sophia will be fine.' He dismissed his sister with a coolness that told Cherry he hadn't forgiven Sophia yet. Something his next words confirmed. 'She has got what she wanted, after all. To be Santo's wife. Never mind the *furore* her determination has caused.'

'That's a bit hard,' Cherry protested.

'No. It is facing the truth. The Carella strength of mind in action—always getting what it wants.'

'*You're* a Carella,' she pointed out, knowing he was right and that Sophia had been determined to have Santo all along. 'Do you always get what you want?'

He smiled—a smile as predatory as the women he'd spoken of a few minutes before. 'Always,' he said softly, slanting a glance at her that—although mockingly teasing—was interested to see her reaction.

'So it's OK for you, but not for Sophia because she's a woman?' Cherry said, with more acidity than she was actually feeling. If what she'd read in his eyes was right then Vittorio Carella wanted *her*, impossible though it seemed for a man who could have any woman he desired with a click of his fingers. But perhaps it was because she hadn't fallen at his feet in humble adoration that he was interested? she asked herself in the next moment. All those hopeful daughters of predacious Italian mammas had probably been schooled to worship the ground he walked on, and the sophisticated female socialites his wealth would bring him into contact with would have no qualms about stroking his male ego—among other things. She blushed hotly as though she'd spoken the last thought out loud.

'It is OK for me because I am a grown man who can control his emotions and bring sense and reason into any situation,' Vittorio stated with unshakable arrogance. 'Sophia, as yet, cannot. She is capable of acting like a spoilt child on occasion.'

'So you never let your heart rule your head?' she said crisply. 'I find that very sad.'

Vittorio pulled off the road into a square they were passing which was deserted in the hot afternoon sun now the siesta had begun, apart from the odd pigeon pecking around. Without a word he cut the engine and moved to take her into his arms, pulling her into him as he took her lips in a scorching kiss. Like the time at the pool the day before she didn't even think about objecting, instead savouring his closeness, drinking in his elusive unique scent—a combination of freshly laundered clothes, the clean shampoo fragrance of his hair and the delicious aftershave he wore. His body was strong and solid, as intoxicating as the powerful aura of masculinity that surrounded him, and his body heat enveloped her so it felt as though they were the only people in the world.

As the kiss deepened her mouth opened willingly under his, her arms slipping up and around his shoulders. She heard his sharp intake of breath as she ran her fingers through the crisp dark hair at the base of his head and knew he was aroused. The knowledge ignited a desire more powerful than anything she'd felt before.

How long the kiss lasted she had no idea. The flames of hot pleasure were taking over time and reality and her nerve-endings were sensitised to screaming point. His hands were stroking her body, and although she knew she should stop this, her need of him was stronger than her will-power, stronger than reason.

It was the car horn blaring as Vittorio shifted position that broke the spell. He swore, softly and fluently, in his native tongue, before muttering, 'This is ridiculous. I have not made love to a girl in a car since I was sixteen and borrowed my father's Ferrari for the purpose.

It was uncomfortable then and it's uncomfortable now.'
He eyed her wryly. 'This is what comes of letting one's
heart rule one's head, *mia piccola*.'

Cherry stared at him, struggling to bring her whirling
brain to order so she could match his cool amusement
but it was beyond her. Necking in a car! She could just
hear her mother's voice.

Vittorio settled back in his own seat before taking her
hand and raising it to his lips. He kissed the fleshy mound
at the base of her palm, then let the tip of his tongue caress the delicate, sensitive skin on the inside of her wrist.

She shivered. She couldn't help it. But common sense
was paramount as she tugged her fingers from his. 'Don't.
Please don't. I meant what I said yesterday. I'm not looking for a holiday romance.'

'I am aware of that,' Vittorio said softly, 'but one kiss
is not a romance, *mia piccola*.'

Well, that had told her, Cherry thought, with a stab
of piercing hurt. Say it as it is, Vittorio, by all means.

Before she could say anything, he added, with shocking honesty, 'That is not to say I do not want you in my
bed, Cherry. I do. Very much. But even if you had not
spelled it out for me I would have known you are not the
type of woman who indulges in casual relationships.'

Why? Because she wasn't beautiful enough? her poor
self-esteem asked immediately. He thought she didn't
get many offers?

'Some women can handle such intimacy and move
on with no regrets when it is over. But you are not like
that. This is why you have been fighting the sexual attraction between us which was there from that first moment on the road yesterday. You know this, as do I. It is
useless to pretend.'

The presumption was beyond belief. It was also true, Cherry admitted silently, but she would rather walk barefoot on burning coals than admit it. 'Actually, and I know this is going to come as a terrible shock,' she said testily, 'not every woman in the world would kill for your body.'

He smiled. The wretch *smiled*. And, from wanting him so badly she had been oblivious to anything but what his hands and mouth were doing to her, Cherry now wanted to kick him.

'I'm fully aware of that,' Vittorio drawled silkily, 'but *you* want me, Cherry.'

In view of how she had just responded to him it was foolish to deny it, but she did so anyway. 'In your dreams.'

To her utter chagrin, his smile widened. 'I had you in my dreams last night, *mia piccola*, and although pleasant it is not like the real thing, *si*? But,' he continued, his face settling into an expression of wide-eyed innocence—if a man like Vittorio could ever look innocent—'you are here to help Sophia. I know this. And taking you into my bed would complicate matters for sure. Added to which, I can see you are not ready for such a step yet. Whether because of this Liam—' the name was said with utter contempt '—or because you need to get to know me better first, it does not matter. Suffice to say I understand we need to take it slowly.'

Cherry stared helplessly into the smoky grey eyes holding hers. This was surreal. She'd told him she had no intention of starting anything but his magnificent arrogance made it like water off a duck's back. Furthermore, he was making her feel silly and she didn't like it.

'There is no "it",' she said primly, and then wished she had bitten her tongue. She had sounded unbearably priggish to her own ears, and his chuckle confirmed he thought so too. The current of mutual attraction he'd spoken of flowed between them and charged the air with an electricity that was palpable—and, unfortunately, undeniable.

'We will make the deal, *si*?' he said suddenly, his voice soothing. 'I will behave and treat you as I would my elderly grandmother while you assist Sophia with the preparations for her wedding. No lovemaking, no kisses, OK? But you will allow me to show you my beautiful country while you are here as you cannot work all the time on the wedding. I forbid it. We will be friends. Is this good?'

It was a darn sight better than grandmother and grandson, Cherry thought with a touch of dark amusement. Although how any red-blooded single woman could be friends with Vittorio was questionable. She knew it was beyond her. But as long as *he* didn't know it she could probably act well enough to carry it off. Dubiously, she nodded.

He chuckled again. 'Oh, Cherry, you have the Italian face—do you know this? All your emotions and thoughts are there to see.'

She didn't like that. It made her feel vulnerable. To counteract the feeling, she said frostily, 'You're Italian, aren't you? And I'd hardly say your emotions are easy to read. In fact you're a closed book, if anything, so I hardly think that observation is valid.'

He lifted up a lock of her hair and then let it fall on to her shoulders as though remembering their arrangement. 'But I am not just Italian. I am a Carella,' he said imperiously. 'The normal rules do not apply.'

She opened her mouth to argue, saw the twinkle in

his eye, and shut it again. He might have been joking, she thought darkly, as Vittorio brought the Range Rover to life again, but many a true word was spoken in jest.

CHAPTER EIGHT

WHEN Cherry was to look back on the weeks that followed they seemed like a rollercoaster, full of climactic highs and lows.

Sophia's morning sickness became all-day sickness, and Vittorio's sister rose late and went to bed early, tired and wan and feeling very sorry for herself, so the practical working-out of the ideas Sophia had for the wedding was left almost entirely to Cherry. Fortunately things were relatively simple. The marriage was to take place in the rather splendid church in the next village, and the merrymaking which was to follow would be held in the grounds of the house, with a huge feast, dancing, and a carousel for the children.

Cherry found that at the heart of Puglian life was tradition—in all senses. The prevalence of Catholicism in the region meant that even the tiniest village boasted an often incongruously impressive church, or even a cathedral, and the church where Sophia was to be wed was no exception. It was remarkably beautiful, and Vittorio had written an open cheque for the wedding so the interior of the church was going to be filled with flowers, and the huge arched front door garlanded with the same.

Sophia was to wear her mother's wedding dress, which

had been carefully preserved and which mercifully would fit her without too many alterations, and Santo's sisters' children were all bridesmaids and pageboys—thirteen in all—with their dresses and outfits provided by one of the big shops in the town of Bari, again courtesy of Vittorio's chequebook.

The arrangements were hard work, but Cherry found unlimited money paved the way most satisfactorily and ironed out any difficulties, leaving her with more spare time than she had expected—something Vittorio took full advantage of. He seemed determined to immerse her in his Italy, which was staunchly lived the classically Italian way, in all its interpretations—proud, traditional, family-orientated, and with people of the soil who had none of the fawning attitudes which could be found in places more reliant on vacation wallets.

She'd met Santo and his parents the day after Vittorio had taken her to Locorotondo and liked them immediately. Santo was quiet, even shy, but clearly head over heels in love with Sophia, and his parents were older than she'd expected—his father white-haired and craggy-faced and his mother small and rotund, with a warm, beaming smile.

She was introduced to Santo's sisters when Vittorio took her to Bari for the purchase of the bridesmaids' dresses and pageboy outfits. They met the families at a restaurant where Vittorio treated everyone to lunch before they made their way to the shops, and although conversation was a little difficult—Santo's sisters spoke no English—the women were friendly and kind and made her feel welcome.

Vittorio had hired a firm of caterers for the wedding, and Margherita had offered to take over the selection of the menu, the wines and so on, as well as the supervision of the team—something Cherry was extremely grateful for. The marriage ceremony was due to take place in the morning and the celebrations would continue all day until late at night; she had been quietly panicking at the prospect of organising enough food and drink for the three hundred or so guests.

At the end of her first week at the Carella villa, she sat by the pool late one afternoon, checking off the frighteningly long list she had initially made of things to do. The church was booked, Sophia's wedding dress was being altered by a local seamstress, the bridesmaids' dresses and pageboy outfits were ordered, the caterers chosen, a huge marquee arranged, and the carousel secured for the children. She still had to organise the flowers for both the church and the marquee, along with Sophia's bouquet and posies for the bridesmaids, little gifts for the best man, bridesmaids and so on, a photographer, and several other things besides. But at least she had made a good start, she decided. She lay back on a sun-lounger and shut her eyes, and immediately thoughts of Vittorio intruded.

Apart from the trip to Bari for the wedding finery, he had insisted on taking her out the day before to Trani, a seaside town up the coast from Bari, which in the Middle Ages had been a thriving and important sea-trading centre and was rich with medieval churches and Baroque *palazzi*. She had objected when he had announced his intention over lunch, but within the hour had found herself sitting in the midnight-blue Ferrari as Vittorio drove them swiftly towards the coast.

They'd looked round Trani's seafront fortress when they'd first arrived in the town, which was centuries old, before moving on to the neighbouring cathedral which dominated the harbour with its Romanesque rose-pink façade and elegant belltower. By then it had been late afternoon, and the sun had lost its heat haze. The beautiful building had basked in a wonderful rose light. The cathedral was breathtaking, with its vast bronze doors and exquisite marble columns in the crypt, but it had been Vittorio's face and voice as he acted as her guide which had really had Cherry entranced. He was touchingly proud of his country and its remarkable history, she'd realised, and not afraid to show it.

They had eaten at a seafront *ristorante*—a grand building with immaculate white linen tablecloths and uniformed waiters—and Vittorio had been the perfect dinner companion: amusing, attentive and self-deprecating, making her laugh as he'd told her story after story against himself.

She realised what he'd been doing, she thought now, sitting up sharply and gazing at the blue water of the vast swimming pool in front of her. He'd been beguiling her, whittling away at her defences, getting under her skin. And it had worked. She groaned softly, lying down once again and shutting her eyes.

They had left the *ristorante* when the sky was black velvet studded with a million twinkling stars and the moon a big white ball in the sky, and she had fully expected him to take her into his arms once they reached the seclusion of the car. But he hadn't. Nor had he stopped at a convenient point on the way home or, once they'd arrived back at the villa, asked her if she'd like coffee or a liqueur before she retired. No. He'd just smiled as he had wished her goodnight, kissed her hand Latin-style and watched her as she'd climbed the stairs to her lonely room.

Stop it. The admonition was strong. She had told him she wanted nothing romantic or intimate, hadn't she? And it was for the best. Each day proved that, because each day she was more and more drawn to him. Vittorio was such a *masculine* man: strong, self-assured, even ruthless, but with a tender sensitivity she'd sensed more than once. And it was this, the softer side, that was so seductive. That and the fact that every gesture he made, every move of his head or action, held a male magnetism that was so sexy it made her ache.

It was blissfully peaceful in the Carella gardens, the only sound the gentle buzzing of insects in the vegetation and the subdued twittering of birds in the trees surrounding the pool, but Cherry didn't feel peaceful inside. She didn't think she'd ever know a moment's peace again until she was far away from this place. Or from Vittorio, to be exact.

She was falling for him and there was nothing she could do about it. In fact, truthfully, she'd fallen for him the moment she'd seen him, and even then she'd sensed, deep in her subconscious, that this man could be her Waterloo. She had got over Liam without too much trouble, apart from bruised pride and a definite distrust in the male sex for a while, but Vittorio wasn't the type of man you got over. Not if you'd been foolish enough to give yourself, body and soul. And unfortunately that was the only way she would be able to give herself.

He was looking for a brief affair, a pleasurable sharing of intimacy that would remain as a warm memory once it was over. She understood that. But it wouldn't be like that for her, and no amount of wishing could change the fact that she had to distance herself from him. *Self-preservation.* She nodded at the thought. Definitely.

Yesterday had proved that, if nothing else. She had been longing for him to make a move when they had left the *ristorante*, practically trembling at the knowledge he would kiss her—which was stupid. Stupid and pathetic. Hell, how had she got herself into this mess anyway?

She must have slept, because when the chinking of glasses woke her it was from a dream so intimate it was definitely X-rated. She opened her eyes and saw Vittorio carefully placing a tray holding a cocktail shaker and two glasses on the table at the side of the lounger. He was wearing the minuscule bathing trunks again, his body as brown as a chestnut and the long muscles in his arms flexing as he let go of the tray and straightened.

'Did I wake you?' he asked softly.

She tried not to stare at his hairy chest and the inverted vee running down his flat stomach to disappear in the trunks. 'No,' she lied. She was always lying around him, it seemed. 'I just had my eyes shut.'

He nodded, taking the lounger beside her and pouring them both a pink cocktail before handing her one.

'What is it?' She'd sat up, pushing back her hair.

'A drink,' he said, poker-faced.

She wrinkled her nose at him. 'You know what I mean. Is it another of your concoctions?' By now she'd come to know that Vittorio's cocktails carried a lethal sting in the tail. They appeared relatively innocuous when you were drinking them, but you had more than a couple at your peril.

He smiled. 'This one is nothing more than pink champagne with a shot of Angostura bitters and a white sugar cube. I might serve this when everyone first arrives at the house after the marriage and I would like your opinion.'

She sipped it tentatively. It was delicious, but then

Vittorio's cocktails always were delicious—that wasn't the problem. 'It tastes potent. What's it called?'

Black eyebrows quirked. '"Wicked Seduction"?'

'You can't. Sophia would never forgive you.'

He grinned. 'Then, *mia piccola*, you name it.'

She thought for a moment. '"Celebration".'

He sighed. 'Boring.'

But that was just it. That was the difference between them. She was run-of-the-mill and the sort of person who would call a cocktail 'Celebration'; he was anything but run-of-the-mill, hence 'Wicked Seduction'.

She shrugged to hide what had felt like a punch in the stomach. 'You did ask.'

'*Si*, this is true. OK, Cherry. Sophia's cocktail is named "Celebration". Now, finish yours and I will pour you another. Maybe after two you will prefer my name?' He turned his head to look at her fully and her breath caught in her throat at his handsomeness.

Somehow she managed to keep her voice light. 'One is more than enough, thank you. I need to keep a clear head. There's still masses to do for the wedding and—'

'And you must have fun too. This was part of the deal, was it not? So we will sit and drink cocktails and watch the sun go down before I take you out to dinner. There is a place I know where the food is good and the dancing even better. One friend showing another a good time. That is all.'

Cherry shook her head. 'I don't think so, Vittorio.'

'*Si*. I think so.' His grey eyes scanned her face. 'We will eat and dance and forget all about the wedding for a while, and you will be refreshed to begin work again tomorrow.'

Did he know she was fighting herself even more than

him? That there was nothing more she would like than to spend the evening with him, which was exactly why she mustn't? 'We said—'

'I am being very good.' He interrupted her again, but this time his voice was unashamedly cajoling. 'I do not make love to you, as I would like. I am keeping my promise, so this is my reward. We will spend the evening together, away from lists and plans and schedules. OK?'

She might have still been able to resist if he hadn't leaned over and taken her free hand, lifting it to his mouth and kissing the pulse beating in her wrist. She stared down at the dark head and knew she was lost.

He settled back on his lounger, letting go of her fingers. 'OK?' he said again.

She nodded weakly. Which wasn't the way to deal with someone like Vittorio, she knew. The trouble was, how *did* you cope with a man who was as sexy as sin and twice as irresistible?

CHAPTER NINE

A COUPLE of hours later she was gazing despairingly at herself in the mirror in her bedroom. She had seized the opportunity when they'd been sorting out the brides-maids' dresses and pageboy outfits in Bari to buy herself two new frocks, so she didn't have to keep alternating the two dresses she'd brought with her from England each night, but now she wasn't sure she had chosen well. The draped silk-jersey dress in a pale peach had seemed perfect in the shop, but now she wondered if the neck-line was a little too plunging and the material a trifle too clingy. And her other acquisition, a red shot-silk chiffon dress, seemed to scream *look at me*, and she didn't want Vittorio to think she was trying too hard.

Whatever had possessed her? She sat down with a lit-tle plump on the bed. Both dresses were not the sort of clothes she would normally buy, but in the shop, where there had been rack upon rack of wildly seductive frocks, they had seemed quite respectable. They still were, she supposed, but just not *her*. Mind you, over the last days she had lost sight of who she was. The emotions and feel-ings which had taken her over were far removed from the person she'd thought she was.

There was a knock at the bedroom door, and as she

called, 'Come in,' Sophia came into the room—much as she had done that first evening a week ago. Vittorio's sister had been resting in her room for most of the day, but round about this time every night the debilitating nausea seemed to lift until the next morning. Cherry just hoped it had lessened when the wedding, four weeks away, took place. A bride who was distinctly green about the gills wouldn't exactly add the right touch to the occasion.

'You look lovely,' Sophia said warmly, her hands on her hips as she surveyed Cherry. 'That dress is perfect for you.'

'Do you really think so?' Cherry peered anxiously into the mirror once more. 'I'm not sure.'

'*Si*, it is so. But maybe your hair...' Sophia put her head on one side like a bird. 'I know. Wait here.'

While Sophia had gone, Cherry turned her attention from the dress to her hair. What was wrong with it? She'd put it up in a coil at the back of her head, feeling the elegant dress deserved a more sophisticated style.

Sophia returned with a box of pins and several tiny crystal clips. 'Sit,' she said imperiously, pushing Cherry down on the velvet stool in front of the sleek dressing table before whipping out the clip holding her hair in place. 'I like playing with the hairstyles. I used to do the same with my dollies when I was a little girl.'

Great. Now she was Barbie. Cherry shut her eyes, knowing protest was useless. This was a Carella after all.

After a few minutes, and with laughter in her voice, Sophia said, 'You can open your eyes now, Cherry, and see what a bird's nest your hair has become.'

It wasn't, of course. In fact Cherry couldn't believe what Sophia had accomplished in such a short time. Her hair was caught in a soft loose style that emphasised her slender neck without being too formal, cleverly held in place with the pins which were now invisible and the odd shining coil emphasised by the crystal clips which glittered in the light. It was the sort of feminine modern hairdo Cherry had seen in glossy magazines and imagined it would take hours and cans of hairspray to accomplish, but Sophia had worked her transformation in minutes.

Throughout her childhood and youth Cherry had never been one to make close girlfriends—Angela had always poached them immediately if she thought they preferred Cherry to her—and she wasn't used to the way females could support members of their own sex when called to do so. She had got used to keeping herself to herself, she supposed, but Sophia's genuine affection and friendliness touched something deep inside that brought tears to her eyes.

'It's wonderful.' She turned on the stool, smiling, blinking the telltale moisture away. 'You're a marvel.'

'No, I think it is you who is the marvel for staying to help me,' Sophia said softly. 'And I know Vittorio thinks so too, although being a man he probably would not say.' She took Cherry's hands, drawing her up from the stool. 'Now, go and have a lovely time, Cherry, and dance the night away.'

Feeling ridiculously shy, Cherry followed Sophia out of the room and down the stairs to where Vittorio was already waiting in the vast hall. He had dressed up too—black dinner jacket and tie—and he dominated the light-coloured surroundings with his dark brooding attractiveness. He moved to meet her at the bottom of the stairs, his grey eyes hot and glittering but his voice deliberately gentle as he said, 'You look quite beautiful, *mia piccola.* I am honoured to be accompanying you this evening.'

It was so Italian, so different from what a date in England might say, that curiously it relaxed her. This was a brief, enchanting interlude in her life, something that wouldn't—couldn't—last, but enchanting nonetheless, and just for tonight she was going to enjoy herself. She didn't know it but her smile was radiant.

'Thank you.' Turning to Sophia at the side of her, she gave Vittorio's sister a hug. 'See you tomorrow.'

Sophia hugged her back. *'Arrivederci*—and, remember, have a good time.'

Once in the Ferrari, Cherry turned to look at Vittorio as the engine sprang into life and he negotiated the powerful car in a semi-circle and away from the villa. 'Where are we going?'

'Not too far.' He glanced at her before returning his attention to the road. 'I have a friend who owns a nightclub in Altamura. It is a town eight or nine miles from here.'

'I think I've heard of it. Isn't that where they recently discovered a prehistoric man in a cave, dating back some four hundred thousand years, as well as various megaliths?' Cherry asked interestedly. It had been on her list 'to see' before she left the region.

'Uomo di Altamura, *si*. But we will not be visiting the cave tonight,' Vittorio said drily. 'Perhaps another time.'

She nodded. 'I'd like that.'

He flashed a smile. 'Then it is a date. Altamura, like so much of Italy, has lived many lives and died many deaths, first dominated by one culture and then another, with much blood spilt. But it is this which gives my country its diversity and love of independence, so it is not a bad thing, I think.'

She couldn't tear her gaze away from the proud, autocratic profile. 'You love this country, don't you?' she said softly.

'It is my blood, my bones, my heart.' Again the dark eyes raked her face for a moment. 'But it is this way with most people of every nation, is it not?'

'No, I don't think so,' she disagreed thoughtfully. 'Perhaps it was once, but not now. Modern society seems intent on ripping itself to pieces from the inside out, from what I can see, never satisfied with its politicians or lifestyle, always wanting more, whatever the cost to community or family life.'

'It is not this way in Puglia,' Vittorio said firmly.

She agreed with him. It wasn't. The slow pace of life and sleepy ambience was seductively sweet, and within a day or two of being in the region it had become apparent to her that Italians in this part of the world very much worked to live, rather than the other way round. Along with the custom of the siesta, she'd been charmed by what the Italians called the *passeggiata*—an evening stroll taken by whole families through the streets as the towns and villages awoke and people came together for coffee, an ice cream and a gossip. It was a charming way of life and would be a deeply satisfying environment in which to bring up children.

Determinedly wrenching her mind from following that path, Cherry settled in her seat and looked out of the window, trying to ignore what the faint scent of clean, sharp aftershave combined with a hint of primitive, virile male was doing to her senses. It was a glorious evening, and as the journey got underway the road wound through the inevitable olive groves and vineyards, along with cherry and almond orchards and walnut trees. The sun-baked landscape was peaceful and serene—sunstruck white-walled villas and the odd *trulli* house or two dozing in the warm air, kinder now the fierce heat of the day had mellowed.

She didn't want to leave this heavenly part of the world. Cherry's mind was whirling behind her calm façade. And she didn't want to leave Vittorio either. Admitting that to herself was half the battle in dealing with the emotions he'd aroused.

'You are very quiet.' His smoky voice interrupted her thoughts. 'I have not forgotten our agreement, if that is what is worrying you.'

'I'm not worried,' she returned swiftly. 'I'm just admiring the view.' In more ways than one. He looked good enough to eat normally, but tonight he was devastating. All men seemed to acquire a certain something in a dinner jacket and tie but Vittorio took it to a new dimension; forget James Bond, she thought wryly. He wouldn't have stood a chance with the ladies tonight.

'This is good. I want you to appreciate my beautiful country and forget anything that is not Italian from henceforth.'

Cherry glanced at him to see if he was joking, but the handsome face was perfectly serious. 'That wouldn't be very practical. I do have to go home eventually, you know.'

'Why?' he asked with deceptive mildness. 'To watch your troubled sister wreck more lives? I do not think you wish this. Do you, Cherry?'

She fiddled with her bracelet. She had known this man only a week or so and yet here he was asking personal, probing questions which he must know she couldn't answer. Yet what was even more disturbing was that she wanted to answer him, to pour out her thoughts and feelings, to tell him all about herself. Which would be utter emotional suicide. 'I don't normally have anything much to do with Angela or my mother,' she hedged carefully.

'So you have no real ties in England?'

That wasn't what she'd meant. 'I have friends, aunts, uncles, cousins,' she answered slowly. 'OK?'

'No grandparents?' he persisted silkily. 'No one that close?'

'No, not now. Satisfied?' she asked a trifle tersely.

'And you see these friends and other family members often?'

She frowned, staring pointedly at him. 'Is this an interrogation?'

'Is that what it feels like?' he returned smoothly.

'Please stop answering a question with another,' she said irritably.

'Is that what I am doing?' And then he chuckled. '*Si*, I see what you mean. I apologise. I would like to know more about you, that is all. I feel at a disadvantage. You are living in my house, you are friends with my sister—you know a great deal about me and the life I lead, do you not?'

She stared at him disbelievingly. She knew *nothing* about him. Nothing that really mattered, that was. OK, his love-life, in effect. But even the little she'd gleaned about Caterina had come from Sophia; he'd given her no specifics. Not one.

He waited a moment or two. 'You do not agree?'

She shrugged. There was no way she was going to humiliate herself by asking about other women. 'I think you are a very private person who only lets people see what you want them to see,' she prevaricated uneasily.

Now it was Vittorio's turn to frown. 'You think I have the secrets? Is that what you are saying?'

'Not secrets exactly, no.' She was floundering. 'Like I said once before, you're a closed book, that's all.'

'I do not think this is so,' he said firmly.

'Then we'll have to agree to disagree on the matter,' Cherry said with equal firmness.

They drove in silence the rest of the way to Altamura— Vittorio concentrating on driving and Cherry staring through the window at a view which had lost its interest. The unresolved issue and the way the conversation had gone had made her feel tense and awkward, taking the anticipation and excitement out of the evening and making her feel flat and miserable.

The town was bustling when they arrived, full of families eating out or sitting in the last of the sunshine outside the little *trattorias* and *osterias* and pizzerias which were everywhere.

When Vittorio swung the Ferrari off the road into a large palm-fringed courtyard and cut the engine, he made no move to open the door. Turning to her, he said quietly, 'For a long time now I have taken care of Sophia. It was important after the death of our parents to give her stability and a sense of security, you understand? To try and be all our father and mother would have been and to shoulder any responsibility or difficulties. I think this is possibly why I have become the closed book of which you speak, but it is not intentional. I was betrothed to an Italian girl when my parents were killed—the daughter of friends of theirs. This did not work out, and since that time I have not brought any women to the villa for Sophia's sake. That is not to say that I have not had an active social life, but I have not been used to—what is the English expression?—wearing my heart on my sleeve with anyone. My relationships have been…transitory.'

Cherry listened, afraid to breathe.

'I did not mean to ask anything of you I would not be willing to give myself, or to play the clever games, *si*? There should be no secrets between friends, I feel.'

Friends. Well, it was what she had insisted on. She remained silent, trying to reconcile what she was hearing with the Vittorio she had built up in her mind, and failing.

'I wanted tonight to be enjoyable—a thank-you for all your hard work so far and for taking the burden of the arrangements off Sophia's shoulders more successfully than I had anticipated. I am grateful, Cherry. I wish you to know this.'

She didn't want gratitude, she wanted— She slammed a door in her mind, forcing herself to say as quietly as he'd spoken, 'Thank you, but you don't have to do things like this to show your gratitude. Besides which, I'm staying in your beautiful home and having a lovely time— really.'

Ignoring the latter words, he said fiercely, 'I do not *have* to escort you tonight. I want to, and that is different.' He bent his head quickly and kissed her before she realised his intention. A hard kiss, unapologetically hungry but over in a moment.

Nevertheless, everything changed and the night was magical again as he opened the car door and walked round to her door to help her alight. And this time she refused to acknowledge the little warning light in the back of her mind that was glowing red.

CHAPTER TEN

THEIR table for two was in a prime position at the edge of the dance floor. The nightclub was crowded and clearly popular, but a bottle of champagne was on ice at their table and within moments of their arrival Vittorio's friend, Domenico, was at their side, greeting them effusively as he poured the champagne.

Initial introductions over, Domenico—who was as portly and small as Vittorio was lean and tall—beamed at Cherry. 'I hear all about you,' he declared somewhat dramatically. 'You help Sophia, *si*? Ah, Sophia—so like her mother in looks but with her father's spirit, eh, Vittorio?'

'Unfortunately this is so,' Vittorio drawled drily.

Cherry surmised—rightly—that Domenico was acquainted with the full facts regarding the hasty wedding, but thought it prudent merely to smile.

'And this Santo. He is a good boy at heart, I hear, Cherry? You think this also?' Domenico asked, as though her opinion mattered. 'You think he will take good care of Sophia?'

Taken aback, she nodded. 'Santo's great,' she said warmly, 'and I'm sure they'll be very happy together.'

'This is good. I would not like my old friend to go grey before his time, eh, Vittorio?' Domenico gave a belly laugh. Then, turning to Cherry again, he added, 'He has been the best brother a sister could have, but now he needs to find a good woman and have plenty of *bambini* to keep him busy, eh? What do you say, Cherry?'

'She says she does not think my private life is any of your concern,' Vittorio interrupted, but without heat. 'You look after Maria and your own *bambini* and leave me to sort out my own life.'

Domenico grinned, clearly not offended. 'Talking of which, there will be a new arrival just after Christmas,' he said contentedly. 'Or an early Christmas present, perhaps.'

'Another?' Vittorio stood up and hugged his friend before saying to Cherry as he sat down again, 'This will be *bambino* number seven. I am surprised Maria has not insisted on separate bedrooms before this.'

'It is Maria who has set her heart on a girl,' Domenico protested. 'She has had the name chosen for the last three pregnancies. Crista Maria, and she will be beautiful.'

'You have six boys?' Cherry stared at Domenico in amazement.

'*Si.*' Domenico couldn't hide his pride. He was clearly an out-and-out family man. 'You like children, Cherry?'

Somewhat bemused, she nodded, sipping her champagne.

'Then Vittorio must bring you to meet them one day soon, *si*? Maria, she will be pleased to show her *bambini* to you.'

Cherry smiled and nodded, but again said nothing. She was beginning to wonder if Vittorio's friend had got the wrong idea about her staying at the Carella villa and her relationship with its charismatic owner.

After a few more words Domenico disappeared, and

Vittorio leaned forward and touched her hand. 'He does not mean anything. He is the good friend, that is all,' he said softly. 'Do not be concerned, Cherry.'

She wasn't exactly concerned. In fact she had been wishing that things were different—that this was a real date, that she was a nice Italian girl, the sort of woman Vittorio was eventually bound to marry, being so fiercely Latin. She forced a smile. 'I think your friend is charming,' she said with patent sincerity. 'He clearly thinks the world of you.'

Vittorio smiled back. 'We have been through some good and bad times together,' he agreed quietly. 'Domenico lost his parents and brother when he was a small child and came here from San Severo to live with his grandparents. But he spent most of his time with my family when we became friends. He is more than a friend, he is like a brother, and the three of us—Domenico, another friend, Lorenzo, and myself—were inseparable. It is good to have such friends, I think.'

Lorenzo. That was the man who had married Vittorio's fiancée, wasn't it? The thought was barely there when Vittorio's eyes narrowed as he glanced at a point over her shoulder and swore very softly under his breath.

Before Cherry could even turn her head she was aware of a blast of heavy sickly perfume as a woman came up behind her and paused at their table. 'Vittorio…'

The woman was beautiful, dark and glossy, and very Italian. Her cocktail dress in vivid peacock-blue fitted every curve and dip of her fabulous body, and the plunging neckline was so daring it made Cherry wonder what on earth she'd been worrying about earlier. She watched as Vittorio rose to his feet, at which point the woman literally draped herself all over him, and then became aware of the tall, good-looking man who was with her.

Vittorio disentangled himself with polite firmness, kissed the woman coolly on both cheeks and then reached out and took the man's hand with genuine warmth. 'Lorenzo, how are you? May I introduce my guest? This is Cherry—she is staying at the villa for a while. Cherry, this is my good friend Lorenzo Giordano, and his wife, Caterina.'

She had known. Even before he had said the name she had known it was her. Cherry pulled herself together and somehow managed to smile naturally and speak calmly. 'How do you do?' she said, purposely looking first at Caterina, who was staring at her with hostile amber-brown eyes. When the other woman merely inclined her head, Cherry showed no reaction, turning to Lorenzo and adding, 'So you are the third of the three muske-teers? Vittorio has told me about you and Domenico and himself.'

Lorenzo smiled, showing even white teeth, and then took her hand and raised it to his lips in a gesture of re-spect. 'It is very good to meet you,' he said, as though he meant it. 'Vittorio mentioned you were staying with him while you are in our beautiful country. I am sure Sophia appreciates a female friend to help her with all the preparations for her wedding.'

So Vittorio was still close enough to his friend to have spoken to him about Sophia's wedding and her part in it. Had he explained the full story? But that didn't matter.

Cherry smiled back at Lorenzo, liking him as much as she disliked his wife. 'I'm having a wonderful time,' she said warmly. 'Sophia and I are spending Vittorio's money as though it's water and he never objects.'

'You are staying at Casa Carella?' It was clearly news to Caterina. Unwelcome news. 'You did not tell me this,' she said to her husband, her voice clipped.

Lorenzo shrugged. 'It must have slipped my mind,' he said flatly, his countenance changing as he looked at his wife.

Silence reigned for an infinitesimal moment—an awkward moment, full of things unsaid.

She still loves Vittorio and Lorenzo knows it. Cherry felt as though a bucket of cold water had just been poured over her head, but she had no time to dwell on the revelation because Vittorio was saying cordially, but in a manner which made it clear the conversation was at an end, 'Enjoy your evening,' as he resumed his seat without glancing at Caterina again. 'I will speak to you tomorrow about the new contract,' he added to Lorenzo, again with a warm smile.

His friend nodded, taking Caterina's arm and virtually pushing her forward when she would have remained at their side. As the couple walked to a table on the other side of the dance floor, Vittorio said quietly, 'Lorenzo has an export business and he and I work together on occasion.'

Cherry didn't know what to say. Ridiculously she felt like crying. Caterina was everything she wasn't—beautiful, elegant, sophisticated and quite stunning—totally the sort of woman she would expect Vittorio to be with, in fact. And it had been Caterina who'd left him when he wouldn't send Sophia off to be cared for by relatives—did he still love her deep down? It was possible. More than possible. Was Caterina the real reason he hadn't settled down with someone else?

Drawing on every scrap of her will-power, she managed a smile. 'He seems nice.' It was weak but it would have to do.

'He is.' Vittorio hesitated for a second. 'The Italian girl I spoke of earlier—the one I was betrothed to—she married Lorenzo after we had gone our separate ways.'

She wanted to ask if he'd minded, although it was too personal. She asked anyway. 'That must have been difficult for you.'

'It was awkward for a time.'

When he didn't elaborate, she felt compelled to say, 'She is very beautiful.'

'*Si*, Caterina is beautiful.' There was another silence.

His attitude was confirming all her fears, but now a welcome flood of pride was welling up, stiffening her back and banishing the momentary weakness of tears. She was blowed if she was going to ask him anything more. He clearly didn't want to talk about it and that was fine—just fine. She was just the hired help after all, and—as he'd already made clear—outings like this one were payment for her services to his sister.

She raised her head, glancing round the room as she said, 'This is a fabulous place. Domenico has clearly made a success of the business.'

'Cherry—'

Whatever Vittorio had been about to say was interrupted by the waiter bustling up to their table, exchanging pleasantries with Vittorio, who clearly was a regular visitor, then placing two embossed menus in their hands, before topping up their glasses although Vittorio had barely touched his.

Feeling in need of some sustenance, Cherry took a healthy gulp. She was going to get through this evening with a smile on her face and dignity intact, no matter what, she told herself grittily. She couldn't compete with an out-and-out beauty like Caterina and she wasn't going to try.

She was facing the table where Lorenzo and Caterina were sitting. Lorenzo was sideways on, but Cherry noticed Caterina had positioned herself so she had a clear view of them, and that the Italian woman had barely taken her eyes off her since she'd sat down. Deliberately now she glanced across the room and met the amber-brown gaze. She didn't smile, and neither did Caterina, and for a few moments their gaze interlocked. Then Lorenzo's wife lowered her eyes, her face stormy.

It was a small victory, but a victory nonetheless. The waiter had made himself scarce presumably to give them time to choose, and Vittorio said quietly, 'Would you like me to order for you?'

She glanced at the menu. It was in Italian and there were no prices. Great. 'Thank you.' She kept her voice polite and light. This evening was just getting better and better, she thought a trifle hysterically. It only needed Angela and her mother to appear like genii out of a bottle to emphasise she was totally out of her depth and didn't belong here.

She found she had drained her glass without meaning to, and as Vittorio filled it with the sparkling champagne she warned herself to restrain from drinking any more until she had had something to eat. If ever she needed to keep her wits about her, it was tonight.

'Perhaps *cannelloni ripieni* to begin with,' Vittorio suggested. 'It is particularly good here. Or *parmigiano di melanzane*—aubergine baked with cheese and tomato sauce. It is a local speciality. And lobster to follow I think.'

Cherry nodded. She didn't care what she ate. Since Caterina had arrived she'd lost her appetite.

The waiter reappeared with a plate of olives and anchovies, warm bread and fine olive oil for dipping for them to share, and then bustled off again after taking their order.

A small band was playing melodious Latin music at the back of the dance floor on a tiny raised stage, and already a few couples were dancing. Everyone was having a wonderful time, she thought bitterly—and then she froze in horror as Vittorio stood in one fluent movement and held out his hand to her.

'Shall we?'

She stared at him, knowing it was quite beyond her to be on show to the rest of the diners—something the couples who were dancing seemed to be enjoying. She wasn't Italian. She didn't know all the Latin moves. But neither could she leave Vittorio standing there.

Somehow she found she was on her feet, and immediately Vittorio's arm was round her waist and he had pulled her into him, holding her firmly and confidently as they began to dance. 'Relax,' he murmured softly against her hair. 'It is not difficult. Just follow my lead. OK?'

So not OK. She was going to make a fool of herself. She knew it. And then the fact that she was in his arms, her body moulded to his like a second skin, took over. Her reactions came automatically, naturally, and the feel and smell of him took her into a sensually satisfying world where the couples around them ceased to exist.

Vittorio was an excellent dancer in every way. No woman could fail to look graceful as his partner. It was the easiest thing in the world to follow his lead as he'd asked. She just let the powerful masculine body move and guide her. A slow, dreamy number began and he drew her closer still, her face nestled under his chin, and her arms sliding up around his neck. She breathed him in, intoxicated not by the champagne but by his nearness. She could stay like this for ever, she thought wildly.

She felt the unmistakable hardening of his body and knew he was as aroused as she was, but his control was absolute. He didn't falter in his steps, whereas by the time they had reached their table and he had gently delivered her into her seat her legs felt like jelly.

Their first course was waiting for them; Vittorio had obviously seen the waiter bring the dishes to the table, but for a moment Cherry stared at the aubergine blankly, her breathing still heavy and slow and her body aching with desire.

How could this man inspire such a flood of blistering sensation just by holding her in his arms? she asked herself faintly. He hadn't been making love to her, they had been dancing, and yet…

'Try it. It is good.'

His deep voice interrupted her chaotic thoughts, and when she lifted her head and looked at him she saw he was tucking into his meal with every appearance of enjoyment. For a moment it took all her will-power not to kick him—hard. Here was she, in a state of virtual collapse, and he was sitting there filling his belly as if nothing had happened.

And then he looked straight at her and she read a hunger in the glittering grey eyes which had nothing to do with food—something the slash of red colour across the high chiselled cheekbones confirmed. He wanted her. He was merely better at hiding it than she was. For the life of her she didn't know if that made her feel better or worse.

The *parmigiano di melanzane* was good, as was the lobster which followed, and the dessert—a sticky pastry confection full of cream, jam and almonds—melted in the mouth. Amazingly, Cherry found she'd relaxed a few mouthfuls into the meal. Mainly because Vittorio had put himself out to make her so. He had the ability to make it seem as though there was just the two of them in a crowd of people. She purposely didn't look at Caterina again, and as a party of four had come to sit at the table next to the other couple, which blocked her view somewhat, this wasn't difficult.

From having no appetite at the beginning of the evening she ate a hearty meal, and when the waiter brought a selection of local cheeses, tiny savoury biscuits, figs and grapes after the dessert, she made inroads into that too. As she sipped the espresso which rounded off the meal, she sighed contentedly. 'I think I've just eaten more than I ever have before in the whole of my life,' she confessed to Vittorio, who was watching her with a slumbering smile. 'I shan't be able to move from this table for days.'

For answer, he drew her to her feet. 'Dance with me,' he murmured smokily. 'I want to feel you in my arms again.'

She didn't argue. She'd been waiting for this moment with little thrills of anticipation.

She was aware once of Caterina and Lorenzo on the dance floor, but whether by design or accident they were not close enough to speak.

It was just after midnight when she made her way to the women's cloakroom—an elaborate affair in cream marble with huge mirrors and small velvet chairs—and Caterina confronted her. Cherry realised she'd known she would.

Cherry came out of one of the cubicles to find the Italian woman sitting in front of a mirror, applying bright red lipstick, and immediately her stomach did a flip. She knew without a shadow of a doubt that Lorenzo's wife had contrived that they should meet with the men out of earshot. The golden gaze surveyed her haughtily before Caterina turned on the chair to face her, her beautifully shaped but thin lips stretching in a cold smile. *'Ciao,'* she drawled smoothly. 'You are enjoying the evening?'

Determined not to be drawn, whatever happened, Cherry smiled back. 'Yes, thank you. Domenico has a lovely place here.'

'Si, this is so. Thanks to Vittorio.' Fine eyebrows rose in the perfect bone structure of her face as Caterina added, 'You are aware that Vittorio provided the money for Domenico to buy the nightclub? No? But then there is probably much you do not know about Vittorio.'

Cherry kept the smile in place by Herculean effort. 'Yes, I suppose so,' she agreed lightly, wondering if it would look as if she was running away if she walked straight out of the cloakroom, and wishing someone else would come in so they were not alone. She wouldn't put anything past this woman.

'You are Sophia's friend, *si*?' Caterina went on, clearly feeling her way. 'How long have you known Vittorio's sister?'

'Some time.' Seven days or so, to be precise.

'And you come to stay to help her with the wedding. It is sudden, this wedding, I think.' There was a definite edge to Caterina's voice. Whatever Lorenzo did or did not know, he clearly hadn't shared it with his wife.

Cherry shrugged. 'Sophia and Santo have known each

other all their lives and loved each other for as long, actually, so I wouldn't say it's sudden.'

The red-painted lips curled slightly. 'No? And Vittorio, he is happy about his sister marrying this...farmer? I thought Sophia was going to finishing school somewhere. That was what Vittorio wanted for her.'

This woman was poison. Cherry had the feeling anything she said would be twisted in some way and used against her. Carefully, she smoothed her hair in the mirror, keeping her eyes on her reflection when she said offhandedly, 'I don't know about that.'

Caterina made a small sound in her throat which could have meant anything, but her voice was definitely venomous when she said, 'And why should you? You are nothing to him. You are not even Italian. Vittorio has many women—beautiful Italian women—but none can keep his affection for long. That is how it is.'

She really didn't want to listen to this. 'Vittorio's private life is none of my business,' Cherry said, her voice now as cold as Caterina's.

'Ha—you do not fool me, little English miss.' Suddenly all pretence at civility was gone as Caterina jumped to her feet, her voice vitriolic. 'I know what it is you want, and you will be disappointed as many before you have been disappointed. Vittorio is the sort of man who only gives his heart once. If you do not know this, you are a fool. And his heart was captured many years ago.' Caterina did not add, *By me*. She didn't have to. Both women were aware of the unspoken words. 'You can befriend his sister but you will not inveigle your way into his life for long.'

This woman was as bad as Angela. Worse. Cherry stared into the angry face which at that moment did not look at all beautiful. Summoning the strategy she'd used all her life for dealing with her sister, she pulled up her emotional drawbridge and took a mental step backwards, her face cool and her voice expressing her distaste when she said, 'Then you have nothing to worry about, Caterina, do you?' And before the other woman could retaliate, she turned and left the cloakroom, stepping into the small carpeted corridor outside and making her way swiftly to the main room of the nightclub.

The rest of the evening was a nightmare. Cherry knew she had retreated into the emotional vacuum she'd perfected over years of heartache and confrontation, but there was nothing she could do about it—nothing she *wanted* to do about it. It was her protection, her safe place. Once she was alone she knew the tears would come, and she'd replay the incident over and over in her mind. It had always been that way. But for now her pride dictated she showed she didn't care. And so she smiled brittle smiles, danced a few more dances, and kept up her end of the conversation with Vittorio, who kept glancing at her with puzzled eyes.

After a suitable interval she said she was tired and asked if they could leave. Mercifully Vittorio didn't walk her across to Lorenzo and Caterina to make their goodbyes, merely raised his hand to his friend across the room, who answered in like manner. Once in the car she feigned sleepiness, pretending to doze on the way home.

Vittorio took her arm as they walked up the steps into the villa, and when they were standing in the hall turned her to face him. 'Is anything wrong?' His dark face was in shadow in the dimly lighted expanse. 'Have I done something to offend you?'

'Of course not.' Her voice was over-bright and she

moderated it as she added, 'I'm tired, that's all, but I've had a lovely time. Thank you very much for a wonderful evening, but now I'd really like to go to bed.'

'No.' When she made to pull away, he tightened his hold on her arm. Not enough to hurt her but making it impossible to extricate herself. 'Something has happened. I know this. You are shutting me out.'

'Shutting you out?' It was too much on top of everything else, and suddenly she wanted to wound as she had been wounded. 'Can you hear yourself, Vittorio? Why do you think you have the right to question me like this anyway? I agreed to stay to help Sophia, that is all. Now, please let go of me.'

'Not until I know why you are behaving in this way,' he ground out angrily.

'Then we'll stand here all night,' she flung back, as angry as he was. How dared he assume he had some kind of divine licence to ride roughshod over people's thoughts and emotions? He had called Caterina beautiful, and she was, but that was just the tip of the iceberg. Underneath his old flame was spiteful and vicious and malevolent, and if he couldn't see that then he was a fool. *But then love made fools of people.*

The thought hit like a punch in the solar plexus, and a truth hammered at the back of her subconscious that she wasn't prepared to acknowledge. Shakily now, and in a voice which was thick with tears, she said again, 'Please let go of me.'

He swore softly under his breath but in the next moment she was free, and like a bird seeing its escape from the cat that was tormenting it she flew across the hall and up the stairs to her room, opening the door with trembling fingers and then turning the catch to lock it once she was safely inside.

Her legs giving way, she slid down on to the carpet and put her face in her hands, wondering if he would follow her and try to speak to her.

But there was only silence.

CHAPTER ELEVEN

CHERRY spent a wretched sleepless night in endless post-mortems, and as a warm, peachy dawn banished the last of the shadows she was forced to acknowledge that she had played right into Caterina's hands. She shouldn't have reacted as she had, she admitted painfully. She had let the Italian woman's poison get under her skin and into her veins. And why? Because already she was far too involved with the enigmatic master of the Carella estate. Vittorio's relationship—past or present—with Caterina, or any other woman for that matter, was nothing to do with her. They weren't a couple. She wasn't going out with him. She had no rights whatsoever.

She watched the sun begin to rise in a cloudlessly brilliant blue Italian sky and faced the unpalatable fact that this fledgling feeling she felt for Vittorio was already aeons stronger than anything she'd felt before. Which meant… Here she faltered. The hard lessons of her childhood and youth and her parents' division—her mother and Angela, she and her father—coupled with Angela's obsessional demands to subjugate and belittle her, and the most recent episode with Liam, had made her shrink from trusting anyone or admitting her feelings. When her father had died she had been inconsolable for a time, knowing the one person in all the world who really loved her was gone, but no one would have guessed.

She cared for Vittorio. No—more than that. She had fallen in love with him in a way that showed her the emotion she'd felt for Liam was puppy love in comparison.

It was the biggest mistake of her life, she admitted soberly, but it had happened, so she might as well face it and get through the next few weeks without burying her head in the sand. And this morning she felt strong enough to mention the altercation with Caterina without the indignity of tears or temper. She would merely say, without going into details, that Caterina had been hurtful and it had upset her, and she hadn't felt able to talk about it last night—hence her behaviour, which she now realised was unacceptable.

Her stomach turning cartwheels at the thought of the conversation ahead of her, she showered and dressed, applying sun protection cream, which was an essential make-up item, but not bothering with anything else, before looping her hair into a shiny ponytail. She was ready long before it was time for breakfast, and went to sit on the sweetly scented balcony, taking a book she didn't even bother to open.

The Carella gardens were ablaze with colour, and for some minutes she simply drank in the beauty stretching in front of her, easing her troubled mind. The brilliant hues of the flowers and bushes and trees against the vivid blue backdrop of sky, the limpid green of bowling-green-smooth lawns surrounded by luxuriant foliage, the warm sun which at this time of the morning was comfortably pleasant, the twitter of birds in the cypress trees which flanked the villa all worked a magic which was bittersweet.

And then the soothing work was abruptly undone as the tall, muscled figure of Vittorio came into view. He was clearly on his way to take an early-morning dip in the pool and was wearing next to nothing—just the minuscule trunks he favoured.

He walked briskly, not looking back at the house, and she felt safe to feast her eyes on the virile male beauty, her breathing becoming quick and shallow. She saw him stop and talk to Francesco, the gardener, for a few moments, and then he continued to the pool, dropping the towel he was carrying on the tiled surround before diving straight in. Unable to tear her eyes away, she watched him cut through the blue water at Olympic speed, covering length after length in the shimmering depths. It was a punishing pace and she sat mesmerised—until she realised he was hauling himself out of the water, at which point she ducked back into the bedroom, feeling as guilty as a voyeur at a peepshow.

It took a minute or two of splashing her hot face with cool water before her colour began to subside, but even then when she looked into the bathroom mirror the lingering sexual awareness in her eyes made her groan. It was acutely humiliating to accept she'd been ogling him like a sex-starved teenager; before she had met Vittorio she wouldn't have said her sex drive was particularly high, but now…

Groaning again, she resumed the splashing for another few moments, comforting herself with the fact Vittorio had been unaware of her lechery. One thing was for sure, she thought desperately once her hot flushes were under control, she didn't know herself any more and she certainly wasn't the woman she'd imagined herself to be. She had expected to fall in love with Italy—everything she'd

read or seen about the country, including its exquisitely
beautiful language, had told her it would be breathtak-
ingly memorable—but to fall in love with an *individual*...
No. That had never been on the cards. And someone like
Vittorio—a man who could have any woman he wanted,
a man from a different culture, a man who was out of her
league in every way.

By the time she went down to breakfast she was in
control again. At least on the outside. She'd made a promise to Sophia and she wouldn't break her word, so that
was that.

Vittorio was alone in the breakfast room, as she'd expected, and without even sitting down Cherry launched
into the speech she'd been practising for the last hour.
'I'm sorry about last night,' she said quickly, before she
lost her nerve. 'I know I spoilt a pleasant evening, but I'd
had a few words with Caterina in the ladies' cloakroom
and it threw me a bit, I think. But that's no excuse, and—'

He'd risen and come to her side. Now he put a finger
to her lips and drew her across the room to the chair next
to his. 'Sit,' he said softly, before pouring her a glass of
freshly squeezed juice from the jug on the table. 'Drink.
Then we talk.'

She took a few sips, her nerves jangling as much at
his presence as the conversation they were about to have.
He looked better than any man had the right to look first
thing in the morning, and again the sheer hopelessness
of the situation threatened to overwhelm her.

'Now.' He took the glass from her nerveless fingers
and placed it on the table, then looked at her seriously.
'Tell me what Caterina said to you, *mia piccola*.'

'It doesn't matter.' She was definitely not about to re-
peat it. It was too embarrassing and degrading—besides

which, it might put the idea in his head that she was trying to ensnare him in some way, as Caterina had intimated. 'Suffice to say she doesn't like me staying here and helping Sophia. I think she takes it as some kind of personal insult because I'm not Italian.'

He tilted her chin with one finger. 'Tell me exactly what she said,' he repeated.

She'd rather be hung, drawn and quartered. She stared straight back at him. 'No,' she said, very firmly.

'It clearly upset you a great deal, so I insist,' he said with equal firmness.

She jerked her chin free and leaned back, away from him. 'I've told you the gist of it. I can't remember word for word.'

He must have realised this was one battle he wasn't going to win because he stared at her for one more moment before swearing under his breath. 'You are the most exasperating woman I have ever met, do you know this?' he grated irritably. 'You look all of sixteen years old this morning, with the horse tail, and yet you are formidable.'

'It's a ponytail,' she corrected, ignoring the rest of what he'd said. She wasn't sure if she liked being called formidable, but she could live with exasperating—although *sixteen*? For a moment Caterina's lush, ripe curves were on the screen of her mind and she inwardly winced. Still, she'd never pretended to be a *femme fatale*.

'Ponytail, horse tail, it is the same.' He stared at her before standing up and taking her hand, and in answer to her surprised look he said, 'We will walk in the garden for a few moments before we eat. I want to talk to you about Caterina in private,' he added, pulling her to her feet.

'You don't have to—' she began, but he wasn't listening.

Once out in the scented sunshine he still held her fingers, and, her heart thudding fit to burst, she glanced up at the hard profile as he began to speak. 'Caterina is the wife of my friend, and for that reason it would be disrespectful to Lorenzo if we were overheard,' he said, sounding very Italian. 'It is not a happy union. I do not think Caterina is capable of making any man happy, and I know that I, myself, had a fortunate escape many years ago when we parted. It did not take me long to realise that what I'd felt for her was not love but something altogether more earthy. When one is young the desires of the body are paramount. And also, perhaps, when one is not so young. This understanding was timely. It has governed my life since. Do you understand what I am saying?'

She hesitated. 'That sexual desire is not love?' And, she reasoned painfully, that he wasn't about to get caught in the trap of committing to any one woman again.

'Just so. But back to Caterina. Lorenzo is a good husband. I say this not just because he is my friend but because I know it to be true. He has remained faithful to her despite extreme provocation; she has had many lovers,' he said grimly. 'But she is Lorenzo's wife, and for that reason I tolerate her; not to do so would mean I lose my friend, *si*?'

Cherry nodded. They had come to a fork in the path they were following and now they turned back towards the house.

'Caterina had no right to comment one way or the other on your presence in my home, and I wish you to forget anything she said. Will you do that, Cherry?' He stopped, drawing both her hands to his chest as he looked down at her. 'It is important.'

She nodded breathlessly whilst knowing it was impossible.

'This is good.' He kissed her mouth, a controlled, swift kiss that left her aching for more as he turned and tucked her hand through his arm. 'So now we will eat, *si*?' he said, with male satisfaction that everything had been sorted.

But it hadn't. For her. In fact Cherry was even more aware that the gap between them was immense and insurmountable. Vittorio's experience with Caterina had soured him to the idea of love. For him everything was about sexual gratification and affairs which carried no commitment beyond having a good time and enjoying each other's company and bodies. She believed him absolutely when he said he knew he'd had a lucky escape over Caterina, but the way that experience had turned out, and Caterina herself now, in the present, only could confirm to him the wisdom of staying footloose and fancy-free.

If she was just interested in fulfilling her physical needs and sating this sexual hunger that smouldered between them every minute of every day that would be fine. Lots of women the world over would be satisfied doing that without making an issue of it. But she wasn't one of them. To make love with a man she would have to give herself body and soul. It was the way she was. It would be for ever. And she couldn't deny the prospect wasn't scary. If she was being brutally honest she knew her parents' marriage had been miserable some—probably most— of the time, and the thought of bringing up children in the atmosphere she'd been raised in was abhorrent. And Vittorio was from a different country, a different culture.

Besides which, he'd always been fabulously wealthy and wildly handsome. Whereas she was just…her. The odds against anything permanent working for them were astronomically high—

Cherry caught at the thought, angry with herself that she had even allowed it into her consciousness. There was no question of Vittorio wanting her for anything more than a brief fling. She knew that. *She knew it*, she told herself with ruthless honesty. And even that would be a disaster. She wasn't sexually experienced, like his other women, and wouldn't have a clue how to keep him interested in bed.

'We are still friends?' He stopped her just before they went inside the house, his rich, deep voice like warm honey.

She looked at him with veiled eyes. 'Of course.'

'Then tomorrow I take you to see the Grotte de Castellana,' Vittorio said firmly. 'The stalagmites and stalactites, *si*? Sophia has told me you are interested in such things, and the history of my country. And there is the museum in Taranto, and the Messapian walls in Manduria, and so much more. We will see it all over the next weeks, I promise this. Together, *si*? Together, *mia piccola*.'

Cherry felt a fresh riot in her stomach. She didn't know how much togetherness she could stand before she threw away her morals and her pride, together with her reason, and begged him to take her on whatever terms he decreed. 'That—that isn't necessary,' she stammered.

His smile was merely a twitch. 'It is necessary for me, and I think a little for you. I want to be with you, Cherry. I am jealous at the thought that you would see these things with someone else, or even just without me. And I will behave myself, OK? I know you do not trust me yet, it is there in those big sad eyes, but time will take care of that. And I will not make love to you until you trust me.'

'Make love to me?' she echoed feverishly. 'I thought we had agreed there is no question of that. I'm staying to help Sophia. I don't want—'

'Then let me do the wanting for both of us.'

And before she could respond to such an outrageous breaking of the rules he kissed her—and no chaste, quick kiss either. His tongue and lips took her by storm as one kiss ran hotly into the next, and by the time he lifted his head she was trembling.

'You—you said no kissing,' she said shakily. 'It—it was part of the deal.'

'This is a new deal.' He smiled a wicked smile. 'Now kissing is allowed. It has to be so. A thirsty man must at least have a drop or two of life-sustaining liquid if his parched frame is to survive.'

The sheer ridiculousness of such a dramatic statement made her lips turn upwards.

His smile widened. He sensed victory. 'Come and eat,' he said softly, drawing her into the house. 'And tomorrow we have the day together.'

It was the first of many such days over the next few weeks as the wedding drew nearer, and each one was a sweet torment.

Puglia was rich in history but its still-small tourist infrastructure meant that its traditional southern Italian lifestyle remained unchanged. There were places where the inhabitants were somewhat bemused by a foreign presence, and Cherry realised that in seeing the country with Vittorio she had the best of both worlds.

He broke the sightseeing with days at the coast a few times, knowing exactly where to go for privacy. East of Gallipoli they found quiet sandy coves where they had stretches of golden sand all to themselves, sharing luncheon picnics Gilda had prepared once they'd swum in the cold salty water, and having dinner in simple but superb seafood restaurants, where the menus were as fresh as the day's catch, before returning to the villa as a deep twilight began to fall.

The first time they spent such a day together Cherry was on tenterhooks the whole time. Vittorio didn't seem to realise how overwhelmingly intimidating his masculinity was, how magnificent, but she found it impossible to behave naturally with his practically naked body on show. The swimming costume she had bought in Bari to replace the one she considered scandalously transparent seemed scant protection against the burning desire no amount of swimming in the icy cold water could quench, but to her chagrin Vittorio didn't seem similarly affected. She had imagined after that scorching kiss in the garden that she would be fighting him off half the time, but although he wasn't shy of physical contact—taking her hand, putting his arm round her, kissing her and holding her close—he was studiously correct when they were alone. And it rankled. Deeply. Which was the height of inconsistency, she knew, and terribly unfair, but there it was. That was how she felt and she didn't seem to be able to do anything about it.

On the days she didn't see Vittorio, she and Sophia worked on the wedding arrangements. The marriage was to take place in the first week of July, and although Vittorio had spent a great deal of money, and with family and friends there were to be over three hundred guests, it was to be very much a casual, family-orientated affair, with none of the strict timetables a wedding in England necessitated.

As the time drew nearer, Cherry knew she would have to make arrangements to leave the villa. She had promised Sophia to stay for the wedding, but had decided to leave the day after the nuptials. To that end, she dug out the paperwork relating to the hire car firm she'd used and asked them to deliver a car to the Carella estate the morning after the wedding. She didn't mention this to either Vittorio or Sophia, but in a strange, heart-wrenching kind of way she felt better once she'd made the phone call. She had taken the bull by the horns and faced reality, crucifyingly painful though it was. The magic interlude was nearly at an end, and although she didn't know how she was going to bear it she would. There was no other option.

CHAPTER TWELVE

THE last week sped by. She met Vittorio's grandmother for the first time—the old lady had been ill for some weeks with a stomach complaint and not up to visitors, but was now recovered—and found her to be an indomitable old lady, very Italian and suspicious of any foreigner. After meeting her, Cherry could see why Vittorio hadn't given Sophia into their grandmother's care.

There were several minor panics, but no one seemed as agitated as she was—although everyone else was merely concerned with the wedding, Cherry thought soberly. She was coping with the reality of never seeing Vittorio again. He'd be out there in the world—laughing, eating, sleeping, enjoying life—and she wouldn't know. It was too unbearable to dwell on, and she managed to put it to the back of her mind during the day. The nights were a different matter. Then the gremlins came in earnest.

Sophia's morning sickness had gradually diminished to the point where it was no longer a problem, although pregnancy tiredness was still an issue. Vittorio's sister normally disappeared off to bed immediately dinner was over—something Cherry found a mixed blessing in the circumstances.

On the eve of the wedding, after a traditional luncheon

at Santo's home, where both families had got together for
a kind of informal rehearsal and to discuss any last little hiccups, and then an afternoon spent supervising the
decoration of the marquee, the construction of the carousel and the stage for the folk dance troupe and band in
the grounds of the villa, Sophia requested a dinner tray
in her room—leaving Cherry and Vittorio to eat alone.

Cherry couldn't describe how she felt even to herself.
A secret part of her had hoped Vittorio would ask her
to stay a while longer, and although her answer would
have to have been no, she'd wanted him to ask anyway.

She hadn't slept well for days—waking very early
before it was light and prowling about her room like a
caged tigress, full of a restless, nervous energy that made
it impossible to rest.

Vittorio had taken her to a festival the week before,
where Italy's national folk dance, the Tarantella, had been
performed, and as she had watched the couples dancing
in whirling circles, accompanied by quick-beat music
on a mandolin, the frenetic pace had touched something
deep inside. She knew the story of the dance—that in
the fifteenth century local peasant women in the town
of Taranto had supposedly been bitten by tarantula spi-
ders and infected with tarantism, believed to be a poi-
sonous venom that could only leave the body by profuse
sweating.

She might not have been bitten by a spider, she'd
thought wretchedly, as the dance had reached hysteria
level, but the infection she was suffering from was even
more deadly, and if she could have rid herself of it by
dancing until she dropped, she would. If nothing else
she might have been able to sleep at night if she was
exhausted to the point of collapse.

When she walked into the dining room Vittorio was waiting for her, an opened bottle of wine in front of him. Her breath caught at the sight of him. It always did. He didn't even have to touch her for her insides to tighten and begin to tremble.

Forcing a smile, she sat down in the chair he'd pulled out for her and accepted the glass of wine he placed in her hand. 'To tomorrow,' she said, pleased at how light her voice sounded, considering she was dying inside. 'Sophia and Santo.'

'Sophia and Santo.' He touched her glass with his. 'And you too. Your help has been invaluable.'

He was wearing a dark grey shirt, unbuttoned at the throat so a couple of inches of hairy chest showed, and black trousers—a vision of tempting male beauty—and his virile sex appeal had never been so potent. Controlling a rush of emotion that had her wanting to throw herself into his arms and kiss him to heaven and back, Cherry took a big gulp of wine. It helped her to say, fairly evenly, 'Not at all. I've enjoyed myself. It isn't often a girl gets to be so involved in a wedding that isn't her own, and thanks to you I've seen more of Puglia than I ever would have done by myself.'

'To be honest, so have I. I think when one is born in a place it is easy to grow blasé, but seeing it all through your eyes has been enchanting. You are enchanting,' he finished huskily.

But not enchanting enough. For an awful moment she thought she had said the words out loud, but when his face didn't change she pulled herself together. This is the last fence, the last furlong—call it what you will, she told herself grimly. She'd get through it with style. It was second nature for Italian males to flirt and give flowery compliments to any woman from sixteen to ninety. She could handle this. She'd been handling it for weeks, hadn't she?

Maybe, but her departure from the Carella estate and from Vittorio hadn't been imminent, an unhelpful little voice reminded her. They had talked often in the last few weeks. Several times she had shared more than she'd intended, and certainly more than she had been comfortable with about her life thus far, and Vittorio had seemed to open up too, sharing the difficulties and pitfalls involved in not only having to take over a business and financial empire when his parents had died so unexpectedly, but bringing up a baby sister.

She had lived in an emotional maelstrom—one day thinking they were getting on really well and that maybe, just maybe, he was beginning to think of her as different from the other women he had known, and then other days plunged into turmoil when he remained distant and almost cold, particularly when they were alone, like now. But tonight he wasn't cold. She swallowed hard. Tonight desire was plain to read on the hard, handsome face.

If only she wasn't feeling sexual arousal such as she'd never felt before she'd be in a better position to keep a cool head. This sort of sexual desire was something she had read about but never envisaged feeling herself. In fact she had doubted if it really existed. Fool, she labelled herself silently. It existed, all right.

'Cherry? Is anything wrong?' His voice was soft, warm, and she became aware his eyes were stroking her face.

She shivered, she couldn't help it, but passed off the reaction by saying quickly, 'Someone walked over my grave.'

'I beg your pardon?' He clearly hadn't heard what she supposed was a very English expression and looked quite alarmed.

In explaining to him a kind of normality was restored, but she was wishing now she had mentioned her intention to leave the day after tomorrow before. It was only courtesy, when all was said and done, and more than that it stated that she knew how things were, that she expected nothing from him. Ever since Caterina had spat her poison she had wondered, just now and again, if Vittorio thought she was out to get herself a rich Italian husband. In the early days he had been so cynical about the women who were paraded before him with hopeful mothers in the background. Oh, she didn't know *what* made him tick, she admitted helplessly. She didn't know what he was thinking, feeling. The man was an enigma.

Their last dinner together wasn't as she'd imagined it would be. It was her fault, she acknowledged miserably. By the time Gilda brought in the dessert the tense atmosphere was so strong the air practically vibrated. From being relaxed and sexy, Vittorio had changed to warily cool—but then her monosyllabic responses and taut body language sent a message no man could ignore.

He waited until Gilda had served the coffee and left them before he spoke. 'OK, Cherry,' he said quietly. 'Now I know something is wrong. What is the matter?'

'Nothing. Not really.' She summoned every ounce of courage she possessed. 'I just thought you ought to know I'm leaving the morning after the wedding. I've arranged for a hire car to be delivered at eleven o'clock. I thought the night before might be a late one for everyone.'

His eyes never left her, but they changed from smoky

grey to almost black. 'Why?' he asked, in an ultra-reasonable tone that boded trouble.

Reminding herself that he had proved over the last few weeks that he could take or leave her—and he'd decided to leave her—she said quietly, 'The reason I'm saying at Casa Carella won't exist any more. Sophia will be a married woman. It's time I continued with my holiday.'

'Your holiday?' The words were a mini-explosion, and he must have realised this, because his tone was very controlled when he next spoke. 'I did not realise that you were so anxious to leave.'

That was so unfair. Righteous indignation steeled her voice. 'It's not a question of that.'

'No? Then what *is* it a question of?'

'I arrived on your doorstep by accident and you were kind enough to help me. I'm aware of that.'

'Stop making yourself sound like a stray cat,' he said, with unforgivable scorn.

Caught on the raw, she drew in a deep breath. 'I agreed to stay and help Sophia because I wanted to. No one put a gun to my head. I'm not saying that. But it wouldn't be right for me to stay on once Sophia is married. You will want to get on with your life, and I intend to get on with mine.'

'And if I want you to stay? What then?'

She gazed at him stonily. She was glad he was so angry. It was helping her say what needed to be said. 'I am not going to be a notch on you bedpost, Vittorio. I've made that clear all along.'

'So you are running away back to England and perhaps to this Liam? Is he the reason you do not want to stay with me? Maybe you are hoping he will invite you back into his bed?'

Now she was as angry as he was. After all she had told him, all she'd shared, he dared to say that? 'I was never in his bed,' she said icily. 'I've never been in anyone's bed, and I am certainly not going to start with you—so why don't you just click your fingers and get one of the women who I'm sure are lining up to take their turn?'

He searched her face, and then shook his head in what looked like bewilderment. 'Why are we arguing?' He reached forward, taking her hand before she could snatch it away. 'It has been good, these last weeks, has it not? And it could be better. I want you, *mia piccola*. I have never wanted a woman more or waited for one so long, believe me.'

She believed him about the waiting. She could imagine most women fell into his arms like ripe plums and considered themselves fortunate to be there. She took another deep breath and let it out evenly. She doubted she could make him understand, but she had to try. 'It has to be about more than wanting for me, Vittorio,' she said quietly, her anger doused by the knowledge that they really were worlds apart.

He stared at her. 'But you do want me.' It was a statement, not a question, but she answered it anyway.

'Yes, I want you,' she said, even more quietly. 'But not just for a week or a month or even a year or two.' There—she had said it. Caterina's words were ringing in her ears—he might think she was trying to ensnare him, as so many other women had done—but she couldn't help that. 'And I know you don't want that,' she added quickly. 'Not with me. Perhaps not with anyone.'

'You do not trust me? You do not think I would be good to you?'

She gently extricated her hand from his warm fingers. 'You know what I am saying, Vittorio, but for the record I *do* trust you. I trust that you are honest in your dealings with women, with me. You made no promises, guaranteed nothing.'

'This is not true.' Suddenly he was angry again. 'I said I would wait until you were ready, did I not? We both know I could have taken you many times over the last weeks if that was all I wanted.'

'But you wouldn't have done that because you are a man, not an animal—a good man.' She was trembling inside, her face tense. She hadn't wanted it to end like this. Perhaps she should just have quietly slipped away the morning after the wedding and left a letter explaining why? But that would have been cowardly, and whatever else she was, she was not a coward. 'And, like you just said, you knew I wasn't ready for a brief affair before we both moved on. I'll never be ready because I wouldn't be able to give myself without it meaning the world. That's how I'm made.'

'You are saying you are going to walk away without giving us a chance?' He leaned back in his chair, dark red colour slashing his cheekbones. 'Then I do not consider this feeling you say you have for me worth anything.'

It was below the belt, and it hurt, but she wasn't going to let him get away with not facing facts. 'The "feeling" is love, Vittorio, whether you believe in it or not, and chance doesn't come into it. If I stayed it would be for ever for me, whether we remained together or whether we parted. I would always be yours, in here.' She touched her chest above her heart. 'The difference is if I leave now I will be able to get on with my life and still function. One day this might even seem like a beautiful dream. If I stayed you would destroy me. I'm not prepared to sacrifice myself, I guess, or let what's between us now become messy and tangled and dark. Me always wanting more and knowing you're incapable of giving it. You feeling hemmed in—trapped, even. And then the parting. In a few months, a year, whatever. Me...' She shook her head, unable to find words as to how she'd feel. 'And you—guilty, angry, ashamed. Because, like I said, you are a good man.'

'And so you are going to leave? Just like that?'

His expression was dumbfounded. Cherry got the feeling that women didn't walk away from Vittorio Carella. It was always the other way round.

She couldn't do this any more. 'Just like that,' she agreed softly. As though it wouldn't be the hardest thing she had ever done.

When she rose to her feet she half expected he would try to stop her, by word or action, but there was nothing—no reaction on his part. He simply watched her with dark brooding eyes as she walked out of the room.

She had just opened the door to her room when he bounded up the stairs. She turned to face him, her heart pounding.

'If I said I would marry you, what then?' he ground out as he reached her.

For a moment hope flared. But only for a moment. In all her wildest fantasies—and she had fantasised about Vittorio asking her to marry him many times, fool that she was—she had never imagined the proposal would be in the form of a challenge, flung at her as though he were throwing down the gauntlet to an adversary.

She looked at him. A long, straight look. 'Then I would tell you to think again,' she said coolly.

He frowned, crossing his arms. 'Meaning what?'

'Meaning such a marriage would be a disaster. A piece of paper and a wedding band doesn't make a marriage, Vittorio. Nothing would be different to what I said downstairs except you would feel trapped earlier rather than later—don't you see? Don't you understand anything of what I've been saying? I want what you can't give. Not just your body. I want it all. Love, togetherness, children, grandchildren. I want someone who will love me when my body isn't so young any more, who will stand shoulder to shoulder with me against the rest of the world if necessary, who will face joy and sorrow and whatever comes our way holding my hand—' She stopped, breathless and on the verge of tears, telling herself she was *not* going to cry. It would be the final humiliation.

He swore softly. 'Why can't you be like other women?' he growled. 'Why do you have to make this so complicated?'

He pulled her into his arms before she could protest, crushing her against his hard frame with her hands imprisoned against his chest. As his lips fastened on hers they held a fierce hunger that was stronger than ever before, made up of desire and anger. The intensity of it took her aback, and she stiffened in his embrace before the heat of his passion kindled the inevitable response and she relaxed against him with a low moan.

As he felt her yield he made a sound deep in his throat of satisfaction, his tongue searching the sweetness of her mouth, and, unable to resist, she allowed him to penetrate its inner depths. His hands curved round her waist, moulding her against him so closely she could scarcely breathe. His lips were doing indescribable things to her senses, and a slow sweet throb was beginning in the core of her that had her pressing against him even as her mind was screaming at her to stop.

His hands slid down the length of her body to cup her buttocks and he began to move her against his hardness, firmly, slowly, erotically, with a languorous rhythm that made her ache.

She barely noticed that he had moved her into the room and shut the door, and in spite of all she had said, all she knew, she felt no panic, only a desire to get closer and closer to the man she loved. His thighs were hard against hers and his heart was pounding like a sledgehammer as they swayed together in the dark room, her hands moving as hungrily as his over the hard planes and powerful muscles of the male body.

She felt him shudder in pleasure and felt a wild exultation, accepting his hands, his mouth, with no thought of drawing back. No thought of anything besides Vittorio.

When they fell on the bed she was beneath him, but his mouth hadn't left hers for one moment. She felt his hands on the skirt of her dress and the silky material obeyed him instantly, moving up her body so the full length of her tanned slim legs was exposed. As he touched her thighs she was galvanised with such blistering sensation that she arched beneath him in an action as old as time— an action that begged for total fulfilment.

When he drew back from her she couldn't believe it at first. For a moment or two she thought he was divesting himself of his clothes, but he was strangely still, his breathing as ragged and sharp as her own, and when she lifted her arms to pull him back to her he slid off the bed, standing tall and dark in the shadowed room.

It was another few moments before he spoke, and by then she had regained enough sense to pull down her dress and sit up, trembling uncontrollably. He had stopped. Why, why had he stopped?

As though in answer to her unspoken thoughts, he said, 'I will not have you like this.' Despite everything, his voice was steady and controlled, with just the faintest tremor betraying the desire which still had him in its grip. 'I did not mean for this to happen when I came up the stairs. You must believe that. I had no intention of taking your will captive.'

Her brain wouldn't compute at first. She stared at him, blinking, absolutely shattered and utterly bereft. 'I—I don't understand,' she whispered at last.

'I promised myself weeks ago that I would not rush you.' He shook his head, whether in annoyance at himself or her she couldn't tell. 'Your innocence is a terrible weapon, do you know that?' he murmured grimly. 'But, no, of course you do not. That is the problem. You do not play games or act the coquette.'

She had no idea of what he was talking about. All she knew was that he had stopped making love to her. That he was able to control this sexual attraction he had for her to the end. She was that unimportant. She was going to cry, and it would be the final humiliation if he saw.

Somehow she pulled herself together enough to whisper, 'Will you go now? Please.'

'Cherry—'

'*Please.*'

And he went. He walked across the room, opened the door and left. Her breath caught in her throat as she stared across the dark expanse, unable to believe for a moment that he had really walked out.

And then the tears came.

CHAPTER THIRTEEN

CHERRY fell asleep some time before dawn simply through exhaustion, but could only have slept for an hour or two before the burgeoning light of a new day touched her senses. She opened heavy eyes and immediately a crushing weight descended on her heart and mind as the events of the night before surged in. And it was Sophia's wedding day. She groaned, burying her head in the pillow for a minute or two and wishing she could go to sleep again and never wake up.

Enough. She sat up, throwing aside the cotton covers which always smelt of fresh air and flowers. Today wasn't about her. It was Vittorio's sister's day, and all the hard work of the last weeks was about to come together. She had promised Sophia she would help her with her dress and veil, along with her make-up and hair, and there would be a hundred and one things to check throughout the day. She was going to be busy and that was great—work would get her through this day—and then tomorrow…

She couldn't think about tomorrow. She shut her eyes tightly for a moment and then padded into the *en-suite* bathroom—only to come to an abrupt halt as she caught sight of herself in the mirror. Horror-struck, she stared at the demented woman looking back at her. Bird's nest hair, swollen blotched skin and pink-rimmed eyes. Car crash, or what?

It took an hour of hard work, but by the time the sun was well and truly up in a brilliant blue sky she looked presentable. Not exactly herself, she thought, on her final check in the mirror before she left the bedroom, but no one would notice. And all eyes were going to be on Sophia today anyway.

For once Sophia was up enjoying an early breakfast when Cherry walked into the breakfast room. Vittorio was sitting at the table, but Sophia's excited squeal as she saw Cherry and then the barrage of comments and questions that followed took the edge off what could have been an awkward moment.

From that point it was all go. Sophia had turned into a whirling dervish, full of a nervous energy that was at distinct odds with her tiredness of the last weeks.

All the bridesmaids and pageboys were going to be waiting at the church for the horse and carriage that would transport Sophia to and from the church—first with Vittorio, who was giving her away, and then after the service with her new husband. It was the tradition that most wedding parties followed the bride and groom back from the church on foot, with the newly married couple leading the way, but in view of the fact that the Carella estate was some little way from the village they'd decided that Sophia had a legitimate excuse for doing away with this custom—which in view of her pregnancy wasn't ideal.

By mid-morning, when Sophia was ready to leave for the church, Vittorio's sister looked beautiful in the frothy, white lace and satin creation which had been her mother's wedding dress and which suited her dark Italian looks perfectly. Sophia was very emotional, and had cried happy tears on and off all morning, but Cherry found *she* was all cried out. She was working on automatic, saying the right things, smiling in the right places, but always with a churning stomach and leaden heart. Nevertheless, her acting ability was such that Sophia didn't suspect anything was wrong.

Apart from at breakfast she hadn't seen Vittorio, having been closeted with his sister in Sophia's bedroom before hastily getting ready herself, but as she followed the bride down the stairs to the hall—with handfuls of Sophia's magnificent lace train draped over her arms—he was waiting.

It was a nasty moment. She hadn't seen him in his wedding suit and he looked like every girl's Christmases rolled into one—a dark, brooding, wildly handsome Heathcliff who was as sexy as hell.

He stepped forward, taking Sophia's hand as his sister reached him, smiling as he said, 'You look beautiful. Our mother would have been so proud of you today, wearing her dress to perfection, and our father would have felt like a king giving you away. I am a poor substitute, but I love you—you know this?'

The tears had started again. Cherry could tell by the sniff Sophia gave before she whispered, 'And I you.'

Vittorio looked over her head to where Cherry was standing. 'And you too look beautiful, *mia piccola*,' he said, very softly.

It was almost too much. She was holding herself together by a thread. She managed a smile, but didn't trust herself to speak, and then Sophia saved her by turning round and saying, 'You need to go before us, Cherry,' as though she didn't know.

Once outside in the summer-scented air, she hurried over to the car in which Gilda and the two maids already sat, getting into the passenger seat by the driver. Vittorio had hired an army of cars to transport his guests to and fro during the day. No expense had been spared. They were away at once, and by the time they arrived at the beautiful village church she had herself under control again and had vowed that would be the last time she faltered.

The scent of a million flowers filled the interior of the incredibly ornate church, the stained-glass windows lit by bright sunshine and the exquisite wood and stone work shown off to perfection in the glowing golden light.

Cherry took her place among the congregation after checking that all the bridesmaids and pageboys had arrived and knew their roles, smiling at Santo when he turned round to raise his hand to her. He looked scared to death, poor lamb, she thought, a dart of amusement piercing the sadness for a moment. He was naturally shy and reserved, and this sort of grand occasion—especially as he was one of the prime players—was his worst nightmare. Nevertheless, the more she had got to know Santo and his family over the last weeks, the more she had been sure that Sophia would be very happy and well cared for in their fold. And there had been the odd time—just once or twice—when she had seen Santo put his foot down with his bride-to-be over something or other, which had reassured her the marriage wouldn't be as unequally yoked as Vittorio had feared.

The music changed, a rustle of anticipation went round the assembled throng, heads turned and the service began. Sophia looked lovely as she walked up the aisle on Vittorio's arm, and as they passed Cherry drew in a long, deep, tortuous breath.

This was the worst part, she told herself desperately. Once the service was over it wouldn't be so poignant. She felt a pair of eyes on her, and turned her head slightly to see Caterina to the far left of her. They stared at one another for a split second—there was a small, curling smile of satisfaction on Lorenzo's wife's face at what she had clearly read in Cherry's—before Cherry broke the hold of the big-cat amber eyes.

Strangely, the fleeting moment provided a dose of adrenaline straight into Cherry's veins, straightening her backbone, lifting her chin and wiping her face clean of all emotion save that which one would expect at a wedding. There was no way she was going to crumble now, she told herself with iron in her spirit. This was possibly the worst day of her life, and tomorrow, when she left the Carella estate, was going to be worse still, but she wasn't a British bulldog for nothing. The stiff British upper lip might be mocked on occasion, but today she welcomed her heritage.

The service was in Italian, as one might expect, and full of conventions and rituals Cherry didn't know, but overall it was charming—if a great deal longer than the average English marriage service. But then it was over, and a smiling Sophia and a proud Santo were sailing down the aisle followed by their bright-eyed and chattering little army of bridesmaids and pageboys, who had been amazingly well behaved throughout. Once outside in the hot Italian sunshine the noise was overwhelming as folk hugged and laughed and called to children who, having been quiet and still for over an hour, were running and shouting and screaming with gay abandon. Everyone was happy and everyone knew everyone else—Cherry had never felt so lost and forlorn in all her life.

And then Vittorio was at her elbow, taking her arm and tucking it through his as he greeted guests and chatted, using English when he could and introducing her

around. It was an exquisite torture, so bittersweet that
for ever after she couldn't remember anything of those
minutes beyond the smell and feel of him and the hot
sun beating down—along with the look on Caterina's
face, which made her appear as though she'd swallowed
something which was choking her.

On the way back to the villa Cherry determinedly
cleared her mind of everything but the view out of the
window, her eyes picking out the beauty of silver spin-
drift olive trees against the flat blue backdrop of sky, a
bird circling high above in the thermals, and the luxuriant
foliage of the Carella gardens when they entered its confines and the honey-coloured building came into view.
Vittorio had asked her to ride back with him, but she'd
made the valid excuse that she and Margherita and the
maids were needed at the villa, to check everything was
in order and supervise the team of caterers.

He'd stared at her, an intent look, before saying softly,
'You are a guest now. You can relax and enjoy the day.'
Something she'd considered an insult in the circumstances. *He* might be able to forget last night and dis-
miss it from his mind as unimportant, she'd thought as
she had smiled coolly and declined his offer again, *she*
actually had feelings.

She had been back at the house for about fifteen minutes when the bridal carriage appeared, a long stream
of cars following it. From that moment the celebrations
began in earnest, and even in her present state of misery
Cherry was affected by the easy, joy-filled atmosphere
and lazy, leisurely pace of the proceedings. Italians loved
children—Cherry had discovered since being in the
country there was none of the 'be seen and not heard' attitude which prevailed in some countries—and little ones
were everywhere, being scooped up in people's arms,

playing games and running hither and thither, clambering on to the carousel and shrieking with laughter and in some cases fright, and just generally turning the occasion into a huge, happy family gathering.

The call into the marquee for lunch was at least two hours late by Cherry's reckoning, but no one, least of all the caterers, seemed to mind, and once inside folk sat where they wanted to sit, with nothing so formal as place-names to spoil the get-together. The only exception was the head table at the top of the marquee, where the bride and groom, Vittorio and his grandmother and Santo's parents with the best man were sitting.

Cherry had been careful to avoid Vittorio since his return from church, busying herself with this and that and pretending to be occupied even when she wasn't, so when she walked into the marquee and took a seat with a nice Italian family she'd been speaking to, who had a good grasp of English, she was surprised when she found herself being raised up by a firm hand at her elbow.

'Vittorio, what are you doing?' she protested quietly, trying to jerk herself free without attracting notice.

'I was going to ask you the same question.' The grey eyes were stormy. 'Why is there not a place for you at the head table?'

'Me?' She was genuinely taken aback and it showed. 'Why should there be? I'm not family.'

'You have enabled this wedding to take place—besides which I will not tolerate you sitting anywhere else. There is now a setting for you next to me.'

She stared at him, not knowing if she wanted to laugh or cry. This was so *Vittorio*. The most conventional of men, he could sweep tradition and decorum out of the window when it seemed right to him. Hadn't he considered how she'd feel, sitting next to him and on show to everyone? It was almost a statement of intent, and she would be the only one in the marquee who knew it for what it was—kindness. And she didn't want his kindness.

'I'm perfectly all right where I am, thank you,' she whispered, resisting the pressure of his hand to draw her forward.

'Be that as it may, you will sit with Sophia and I and the rest of the immediate family.'

'I will not.' She was becoming aware of interested glances in their direction and embarrassment was paramount.

'*Si*, Cherry, you will.' If he had noticed the attention they were drawing, he didn't care.

'Vittorio, think what people will assume,' she hissed softly, her cheeks burning. 'And your grandmother wouldn't like it. You know she wouldn't.' His grandmother had managed to let her know—in spite of not speaking a word of English—exactly what she thought of the little English girl who had taken up residence in the home of her grandson.

'This is not my grandmother's wedding,' he said, none too quietly, stating the obvious, and when her agonised '*Ssh!*' came, added more softly, 'It is Sophia's and Santo's, and they have both requested your presence with them at the top table, OK? Satisfied? You will spoil their wedding breakfast if you deny them this.'

They were becoming a spectacle, and it was this rather than his argument which forced her to accompany him down the long—endlessly long, it seemed—marquee to her seat between Vittorio and his grandmother. The old lady didn't acknowledge her arrival by so much as the flicker of an eyelash, and Cherry thought Sophia and Santo looked bemused rather than anything else, but she was here now and that was that.

The meal was long and leisurely, even by Italian standards, and the wine flowed—red wine, white, rosé, sparkling and even dessert—all courtesy of the Puglia region and all superb. The climate meant that most Puglian wines had a high level of alcohol, the baking summer sun encouraging a large amount of sugar in the grapes, and long before the meal was halfway through the level of laughter and conversation had risen as the guests had got merrier. Cherry felt herself begin to relax a little. Everyone was busy having a good time, and although there was the odd speculative glance in her direction they weren't unfriendly.

Vittorio talked to her mostly, leaning slightly towards her, his arm sliding round the back of her seat now and again, causing her to tense until it was removed again. He spoke to his grandmother a few times and the old lady answered him willingly enough, even unbending enough after three glassfuls of wine to smile and nod at Cherry when Vittorio mentioned her name.

'What did you just say to her?' Cherry asked him cautiously after this miraculous event. By now she'd had a couple of glasses of wine herself, which was a double-edged sword—on the one hand the alcohol had helped her to relax and loosen up a little; on the other she was terrified of letting her guard down and losing the control she was desperate to maintain. She was vitally aware of every tiny movement of the big male body next to her, even when Vittorio was speaking to the bridal couple or Santo's parents and best man. The day had turned into something of a farce, but she was powerless to do anything about it.

'What did I say to her?' Vittorio echoed softly. 'Just that the wind that blew you across our path was a lucky one for the Carellas. Sophia has had the day she wanted, and a large part of that is due to you.'

'I think that's an exaggeration,' she said stiffly. It wasn't fair when he said such things or looked at her with that fire in his eyes. If he had any decency he would let her alone after the travesty of last night. If she didn't love him so much she could hate him, she thought bitterly, and one thing was for sure: today had confirmed that she needed to put as many miles between them as she could. She had no intention of staying around to be toyed with or mocked, if that was what he was doing. Or even flirted with. Flirting was second nature to Italian males, and Vittorio was Italian from the top of his head to the soles of his feet.

She drank half of her third glass of wine for comfort.

It was getting on for six o'clock before the meal was drawing to an end and the speeches began—all in Italian. Most of the children were taking a late siesta before the evening dancing and festivities started, sprawled across their parents' laps or cuddled up on the knees of relations or friends.

A hot and cold buffet had been organised for seven o'clock, and Cherry was just thinking she would have to have a word with Margherita and make sure the caterers delayed this for an hour or two, in view of the late finish of the wedding breakfast, when she became aware that Vittorio, who was giving his speech as 'father of the bride,' had stopped talking and had turned to her, and everyone in the room seemed to be more awake.

She glanced up at him and then became arrested by the look on his face. If this wasn't Vittorio—if this was anyone else—then she would say the emotion laid bare for everyone to see was sheer unadulterated love, but of course that was impossible.

'I have a confession to make,' he said, looking straight into her eyes. His voice loud enough for everyone to hear. 'I am a stupid man. I say this because when someone is fortunate enough to find something infinitely precious they should treasure it at the cost of everything else.'

After the din of the day you could hear a pin drop.

'I knew from the first moment I saw you that I loved you, *mia piccola*, but I am stubborn as well as stupid. I have been used to living my life by my own rules, and when you didn't fall in line I told myself I only had to wait and in time you would come round to my way of thinking, that this feeling I felt would be as easily controlled as everything else in my life. I wanted no permanent attachments, no commitment to any one woman. This is what I told myself. This is how foolish I am. Because I want and need you for ever, Cherry. I will love you for ever. Nothing else will do. I say this now, in front of my family and friends, because it is the truth and I want the world to know it. But the only person who really matters is you.'

Before her mesmerised gaze he went down on one knee. The only sound was a collective gasp from all the women present. 'Will you marry me, *mia piccola*? Will you love me and let me love you all the days of our life? Will you stand shoulder to shoulder with me against the rest of the world and face the sorrow and joys in the future holding tight to my hand?'

He was repeating the words she had spoken the night before, words that only she knew, and as he did so the last doubt that he loved her melted away. Somehow the unbelievable had happened, she thought, her face becoming radiant with a beauty that made every man in the place envy Vittorio and caused every woman to have a lump in her throat—every women except one. But no one no-

ticed Caterina flounce out of the marquee, her face as
ugly as Cherry's was beautiful.

Her voice so low only Vittorio could hear, Cherry
whispered, 'Yes, please,' and as he rose, lifting her into
his arms and kissing her as though they were the only
two people present, every child in the place was suddenly
awoken as their parents went crazy, whooping and cheer-
ing and clapping in a thunderous applause that could have
been heard miles away. But Cherry and Vittorio were
unaware of it, wrapped in each others arms.

They were married six weeks later at the same village
church. This time the bride wore a simple but exquisite silk taffeta ivory dress and carried a small posy of
English daisies, and the groom a black Nouveau jacket
and black trousers with an ivory patterned waistcoat.
Cherry wondered if it was proper to stand at the altar
on your wedding day with such lustful thoughts, but she
couldn't help it. Vittorio looked so good she had gone
weak at the knees when she saw him.

The church was packed to overflowing again. Vittorio
had flown her relations and friends out from England two
days before the wedding, but Liam hadn't accompanied
Angela and her mother although she had included him in
the invitation. Her mother had confided that Angela and
Liam were 'having problems'. From the way Angela had
batted her eyelashes at Vittorio and contrived to take him
aside when she'd only been at the villa for a few minutes
Cherry wasn't surprised.

She didn't know what Vittorio had said to her sister,
but Angela had emerged from the tête-à-tête flushed and
angry and wouldn't say a word to anyone the rest of the
day. However, she did behave herself on the wedding
day, keeping a low profile and staying out of Cherry's

way—which was all Cherry could have asked for. Her mother, openly thrilled that one of her daughters had made such a brilliant match, suddenly seemed to have decided that Cherry was the favourite, twittering around Vittorio and practically falling over her own feet if he so much as looked at her. It was both funny and sad, and Cherry wasn't sorry that the English contingent were leaving the day after the wedding.

The dancing went on late into the night, and Cherry knew she had died and gone to heaven as she floated in her husband's arms in the moonlight, the party going on around them but their eyes only for each other.

At last their guests began to leave, and she smiled as she sensed Vittorio's impatience as the last few lingered. A perfect host normally, he was being tested to the limit.

They walked into the house locked in each other's arms, and when they reached the master bedroom Vittorio turned her to face him before he opened the door. 'No other woman but you has come here,' he said very seriously, his dark eyes stroking her face in a way that made her tremble. 'I want you to know this, *mia piccola*. I have had many woman, you know that, but I have never brought one into my bed in Casa Carella.'

She touched the silken rasp of his chin where the black stubble made him look even sexier. 'I'm glad.'

She hadn't been into his bedroom before. Since he had proposed Vittorio had been very proper. So proper, in fact, that she had felt like ravishing him more times than she could remember. But he had insisted they were going to wait for their wedding night, even though she knew he found it more difficult than she did.

'You are to be my wife,' he had said, sounding very Italian. 'The mother of my children. It is right that it is so.'

And now it *was* their wedding night. She gazed at him

with huge, wondering eyes and he scooped her up in his arms, opening the door and then kicking it shut behind him as he bent his head to hers. She kissed him back with total abandon and touching innocence, wanting him more than she could have thought possible. Simply by looking at her he could fill her with a raging desire; now he was her husband and she didn't have to dream any more.

He kissed her as he'd never kissed her before, the skill of his mouth and tongue making her realise just how much he'd held back over the last weeks. His tongue teased and caressed, working a magic that had her moaning long before he undid the buttons of her dress. His hands were shaking slightly as he let it pool at her feet, and as she stepped out of it his fingers stroked over her body, lingering on her breasts in their lacy cups. 'So beautiful,' he murmured huskily. 'So perfect.'

He picked her up again, carrying her over to the vast bed and peeling off the rest of her clothes, making small growling sounds in his throat as he let his lips caress and suck her darkened nipples until she cried out in pleasure, unable to contain herself.

She was desperate to feel every part of him against her and tugged at his clothes, helping him undress with fingers that felt clumsy and inexperienced. 'I—I'm not very good at this—'

'I am glad that this is so.' As he kicked off his trousers and joined her again on the bed he cupped her face in his hands, kissing her with a sweet tenderness. 'I am the first. You have no idea what that feels like to a man, and it is more than I deserve.'

Vittorio was a lot of things, but humble wasn't one of them, and for a moment Cherry studied him. When she realised he was perfectly serious all her worries about being inexperienced and inadequate melted away and now it was she who pulled him to her with a fierceness that thrilled him.

When she had thought about their physical union Cherry had always imagined it would be quick, lusty and exciting. It was lusty and exciting, all right, but far from quick. Once he had her in his bed Vittorio became intent on giving her pleasure, touching and tasting and kissing every inch of her feverishly sensitive skin. Hot, sweet sensation had her twisting and turning, digging her nails into his hair-roughened body as she writhed and moaned, and when he found the core of her with his lips and tongue the need to feel him inside her became a mind-consuming craving. But she needed to touch and taste *him* too…

Her love for him delighted in intimacy after intimacy, and as he showed her how to touch and please him she exulted in the pleasure she gave, feeling like a goddess as she let her instinct guide her in a sexuality she'd never imagined she possessed, following him as she'd once done on the dance floor, move for move. But this dance of love was beyond anything imaginable.

It was a long time before he eased himself between her thighs. Her eager wetness accepted him even as he tried to go slowly, aware of her tightness as her body adjusted to its satin invader. 'Am I hurting you?' he whispered raggedly, the muscles in his arms bunching as he raised himself slightly to look into her face.

There had been one brief splinter of pain but now her muscles welcomed his thickness, and in answer she arched for deeper penetration, wanting all of him.

His body responded immediately and he moved harder and faster, stretching and filling her until he possessed her to the hilt in a driving rhythm that took them both into ecstasy and then over the edge, to drown in wave after wave of a pleasure so intense it was almost painful.

She was still trembling and helplessly drugged with pleasure minutes later, when he turned on his side, pulling her against him and kissing her hard. 'You are perfection,' he murmured lazily, kissing her eyelids, her nose, her brow, before returning to her mouth, swollen from passion. 'Utter perfection. How have I lived this long without you? I love you with all my heart, *mia piccola*. You know this?'

Yes, she knew it. She smiled a smile that made him catch his breath with its sensuality.

'Prove it,' she whispered softly, reaching up to take his lips in a passionate kiss that brought his body to instant life.

'Gladly,' he whispered back, a touch of laughter in his voice, but then the smouldering fire ignited into red-hot flames and there was only the language of love. The best language of all.

* * * * *